BELLADONNA'S EMPIRE
PART I
By Rita Lewis

Credits

Editors
Cassandra Sims
Karen D. Neal

Cover Design/Interior
Cassandra Sims

Table of Contents

ACKNOWLEDGEMENTS 4

CHAPTER 1 5

CHAPTER 2 13

CHAPTER 3 22

CHAPTER 4 32

CHAPTER 5 48

CHAPTER 6 58

CHAPTER 7 67

CHAPTER 8 74

CHAPTER 9 80

CHAPTER 10 93

CHAPTER 11 111

CHAPTER 12 118

CHAPTER 13 128

CHAPTER 14 150

CHAPTER 15 159

CHAPTER 16 171

CHAPTER 17 185

Acknowledgements

First and foremost, I would like to thank my Lord and Savior, the head of my life, my everything. I would not be the person I am today if it had not been for Him.

My dear friend, Nichole Grubbs: Thank you for introducing me to my beautiful Publisher, Karen D. Neal. Nichole, if it wasn't for you I wouldn't have known anything about Karen D. Neal. Thank you, girl. I love you!

To my lovely daughters, Ebony Lewis and Quinesha Collins: You beautiful ladies have grown up to be so pretty and I'm so proud of you young ladies. Both of you have given me so much hope, love, and understanding. Thank you both for your continuous support and feedback as I wrote this novel. You've both been there throughout this journey, sharing your thoughts supportively. Most importantly, thank you both for the happiness, joy, and excitement you girls share with me on the publishing of my first novel I couldn't have any better daughters in my life to share this journey with. So, I want to say thank you Eb and Ne, I love y'all so dearly, y'all are my rocks!!

To my mother, Rutha Lewis; my sister, Towana Lewis; my nephews, Christopher Lewis and Antonio Reed: thank y'all for being excited and happy for me becoming an author. Thank you, Nephew Christopher, for that day I told you I was getting my book published and you told me you were so happy for me and that it was a blessing. We've have been through so much, and I will never forget that day you told me that—it meant the world to me, because family is everything to me. I'm so proud of you nephew, thanks!!!

Last but definitely not least, to my publisher Karen D. Neal: Thank you lady for believing in me. Thank you for how you talked to me many nights on the phone, giving me pointers on being a *great* author, and how my story should go. Thank you for being supportive during those long talks on the phone about personal stuff. Boy, we sure had some laughs and cries!!! Thank you for telling me to not be so anxious, thank you for pushing me to be the *best* author I can be, and thank you for just being there— not only my publisher, but also as my friend. Love you lady, Ms. Karen D. Neal.

CHAPTER 1

9 a.m. Saturday morning
Viviana's house…

Viviana stood 5 feet 8 inches tall, and her skin was the color of creamy caramel, and as smooth as a baby's bottom. Her double D breasts were round and firm like melons, and her apple bottom booty was big enough to stop traffic. Built like a brick house, she was thick in all the right places, and any man would want to wife her.

As she lay in her California king-sized bed, she turned and looked at the clock.

"Damn, its nine o'clock!" she shouted, as she threw the covers from her naked body and quickly jumped out of bed.

She stretched and yawned before making her way to the bathroom to shower. The bathroom was tastefully decorated in all white, and the sink and walk-in shower were surrounded by white marble. Viviana lived like a queen, and her huge bathroom was roomy enough to comfortably hold eight people.

Since she'd slept in longer than planned, she only had time for a quick shower. She stepped in, turned the water on, and adjusted the temperature until it was just right. She squeezed some of her favorite scented luxurious shower gel, from Neiman Marcus, onto her bath sponge and lathered her wet body with the sweet smell of vanilla fragranced Creed. When she felt clean and fresh, she turned the water off, dried herself with a towel, and grabbed her Chanel robe.

Next, she headed down the stairs to the kitchen to fix herself a cup of coffee, before making her way to the basement.

Vivian was high maintenance, and even the décor of the basement screamed money. The walls had been gutted out and replaced with European marble, and a leather sectional covered the perimeters of each wall. There was a fully stocked bar, an entertainment center that held a 60-inch flat screen TV with surround sound, and she'd even had a hot tub installed.

A big round marble table that matched the walls sat in the center of the floor, atop a thick Persian rug, and two pool tables sat side by side. At the far end of the room was an oval shaped cherry Oakwood desk that held a money machine and 2 laptops, and although the basement was just as lavish as the rest of the house, she still thought it could be better.

After entering the basement, she pulled the lever on the wall that controlled the lighting of the room. *That's much better,* she thought to herself, as she adjusted the brightness to her liking. She made her way over to her desk, and lying on the floor, were eight large duffle bags filled with money. She took a seat at the desk and turned on the mini money machine, and a huge smile spread across her face.

"My life is so luxurious!" she said and laughed out loud.

Reaching down, she grabbed a stack of money out of one of the duffle bags and loaded it into the money machine. She continued loading the machine until she had emptied all the bags.

After dividing the money in to fifty-thousand-dollar stacks, she put it back inside the duffle bags and took them over to one of the marble walls. Looking at the wall, it appeared to be an ordinary wall; however, when Viviana tapped on it, it opened, and inside was a hidden vault filled with money.

Next, she placed her index finger on a scanner, and using her print to open the vault, she placed the duffle bags inside.

Remembering the time, she turned the lights down and rushed back up the stairs to her bedroom—she knew she would need to dress in a hurry if she wanted to make it to her meeting on time.

The bedroom was all white and very spacious. Her closet had been customized with glass motion doors that opened to a closet filled with designer clothing by Prada, Chanel, Nina Garcia, and Giovanni Armani, just to name a few.

Geesh, I have so much to wear, how's a girl to decide? she thought to herself, as she thumbed through her extensive wardrobe. *Ah ha, I'll wear this one*, she decided, pulling out the baby blue Prada V-neck, pencil dress.

She walked through the closet to the section that had shelves and shelves of designer heels. There were shoes branding from Prada, Gucci, Louis V., Fendi, and even more, all by the most popular designers—coupled with all the clothes, the entire closet was truly any woman's fashion paradise. Selecting a pair of baby blue diamond strap heels by Prada, to match her Prada dress, she exited the closet and sat down at her vanity desk.

With pride, she looked herself over in the mirror and smiled at the beautiful reflection looking back at her. *Now let me put this make-up on and get up outta here…*

When she was done and finally pleased with her look for the day, she held up her wrist and glanced at her platinum diamond five-carat watch to check the time.

"Shit, I'm gonna be late!" she said, "Felix is gonna kill me if I don't go ahead and get outta here!"

She rushed down the stairs, grabbed the keys to her Infinity truck, and headed out the door.

It was 4:15 p.m. when Viviana finally arrived at Luigi's Italian restaurant in downtown Newark, New Jersey to meet Felix. Felix and Viviana had a special bond. Not only was he her right-hand man, but he was also her cousin. He was the one who stayed on top of things for her, and the two were really close.

Standing 6 feet 3 inches tall, Felix towered her. He had a handsome baby face with a brownish skin complexion, and long dreads adorned his head. He was a stay-fly kind of dude who drove nothing but the most expensive cars and stayed iced out in the finest diamonds—he was definitely the kind of man women went crazy over.

Felix saw Viviana when she entered the restaurant and stared at her intensely as she made her way over to his table.

"Where the hell you been?" he asked, looking at his watch.

"Boy, please, if you had to count all the money I had to count, yo' ass would be late too, nigga!" she replied as she sat down at the table with him. "So, what's the deal?" she asked, getting straight to the business.

"Everything is everything, Viv, and things goin' as smooth as planned. No worries, Cuz," Felix assured her as he took a sip from his drink. "All my folks comin' through on time with they money so we straight, ya heard," he added with confidence.

"OK. That's what I'm talkin' bout'," Viviana replied with a serious look on her face. If there was one thing she didn't play about, it was her money, and everybody knew it. "So, what you drinkin' on so early in the day, Cuzzo?" she asked.

"White Remy," he answered. "You wanna glass?" he asked, holding his glass up.

"Hell no, I drink wine, boy. You know I keep it classy, and that type of drink is way too hard for a lady like me," she said with a wink followed by a mischievous grin.

"Yeah, yeah, I know, Viv," he replied, smiling back at her. "Well, I guess I'll toast to the good life by myself then." He held his glass high in the air before taking a big gulp. "To the good life," he said, followed by a playful wink at his cousin.

"OK. Enough playing. We have a lot of business to go over," she said, as she reached inside her briefcase and pulled out her Apple MacBook Pro. "Let's see here...," she paused and powered on her laptop, "okay, we need to go over the bank accounts, and we need to see about puttin' some more niggas on the block to make sure we got enough lookouts."

"It's cool, Viv. I told you I got this," Felix reiterated. "I got a few of my main hitters on the corners, and them niggas be on it."

"I know, I know, and I don't doubt that, but Felix we pushin' a lot of weight. I need to make sure we straight at *all* times," she emphasized. "And I definitely need to make sure you protected 'cause yo' ass the main one on the block, *not* me. I need some true thoroughbred guys who gonna have yo' back no matter what."

She stared at Felix with a stern expression and then turned her attention back to her laptop. Felix nodded his head to confirm he understood. He sat in silence as Viviana switched screens to check her off shore bank accounts as well as the ones she had in the states.

It was Monday morning and Viviana was on her way to her clothing store, located in the mall. The flooded streets of New Jersey's downtown area was filled with people from all walks of life. The sidewalks and streets looked like a circus as people tried to get through the morning traffic rush hour. There were business people talking on cell phones, people flagging down cabs, people with iPads, and everyone was in a hurry.

"Boy, it's crowded out here this morning," she said to herself, as she drove her Mercedes Benz 350 through traffic, headed to the parking deck of the mall.

After finding a parking spot, she got out of her car looking like a million dollars dressed in a cream Chanel pant suit, Chanel cream heels, and Chanel accessories to match. She walked to the elevator and rode it up to the floor her store was located on.

The merchandise in the store consisted of the best of everything; with bags, shades, belts, shoes, clothes, and jewelry from the most expensive designers, Viviana's store had become a success almost overnight.

"Good morning everybody," she said, greeting her staff of four as she walked passed them. Sandra and Sharon were her cousins, and then there was Liz and Tonya, two of her closet friends.

"What's up," Sandra spoke.

"Hey, Viv," Sharon called out from across the room.

Sandra was the store manager and Sharon kept track of the shipments and helped out with paperwork. They were Viviana's cousins, and the two of them had been working in the store since the very first day the doors opened. Viviana believed in helping her family out, but don't get it twisted, she also believed in making sure they worked for it.

After making her way to her office, she sat down behind her desk and turned on her 2 black 27-inch flat screen Apple iMac Pro computers. Sandra followed her and took a seat on the other side.

"Everything is going great, Cuz," Sandra said, filling her in on the important events of the morning. "The UPS guy came and dropped off some boxes and inventory this morning."

"Oh yeah?" Viviana replied dryly.

Sandra handed her the shipping slips and she looked them over one by one. When she was done, she handed the slips back to Sandra, asking her to make copies before placing them in the file cabinet. Suddenly feeling a little light-headed, Viviana placed her hand on the side of her head and took a deep breath.

"You okay, Viv?" Sandra asked in a concerned tone. She stared at her cousin waiting for an answer.

"I'm fine, girl . . . just a little exhausted. I've been making so many power moves trying to keep my money and business straight, I hardly have time to sleep. I guess I'm feeling a little drained today," she told her.

"Well, Viv. . . . I know you're a busy woman, but you also have to make time for yourself and give yourself a break sometimes," Sandra replied.

"I know, Sandra, but my lifestyle requires me to live this way. I gotta stay busy if I wanna stay on top of my game," Viviana explained. "But I understand what you're saying, and I appreciate you being concerned, Cuz," she said sincerely. She rubbed her hand through her hair and sighed heavily.

Sandra stood up from the desk to leave the office. Just as she was about to walk out the door, she turned to Viviana and said, "Take a vacation, Viv! Go see your folks in Colombia for a couple of days. Go, relax! Take some time to yourself for a change," then she smiled at her cousin and made her exit from the office.

Leaning back in her chair, Viviana smiled at the thought of seeing her peeps. *It's been a while since I've seen them. . .* and with that thought in mind, she picked up her desk phone and dialed the numbers to call her aunt in Colombia.

CHAPTER 2

Viviana pulled up to her mother Paula's townhouse in Atlantic City, NJ, driving her black Bentley. She walked up to the door and rang the doorbell.

"Hey, Mama!" she said, once Paula opened the door. She leaned in and hugged her mother as if she hadn't seen her in years.

"Hey, baby, what a surprise," Paula replied with a smile. "I wasn't expecting to see you today. What brings you to see mama on a weekday?" she asked, closing the door behind her.

"Well, Mama… I'm thinking about going to Colombia," she explained, as she followed her mother to the living room.

"Colombia? Why you going to Columbia, Viviana?" Paula asked skeptically.

"I'm goin' to see Aunt Maria."

"Are you going by yourself?" her mother asked.

"Yes, Mama, I am. I hadn't really planned on going and it was a last-minute decision," Viviana answered honestly.

"Oh, OK. I'm just a little surprised, that's all," her mother told her. "But we can talk about that some other time. So, how've you been doing, baby?" Paula asked, briefly changing the subject.

"I've been good, Mama… just working… a little tired though."

"Well, try not to push yourself too hard, Viv," Paula said. "So how has your cousin Felix been doin'?" she asked.

"Felix doin' good, Mama, but what made you ask about him?" Viviana replied curiously.

"Well, baby… his mama has been ringin' my phone off the hook. She sounded like she was worried about him."

"What? Worried? Felix is fine, Mama. He just been busy runnin' around for me, that's all," Viviana explained.

Paula became silent for a moment, and Viviana could tell by the look on her face that there was something else she wasn't telling her.

"What is it, Mama?" she asked, noticing the serious look on her mother's face.

"Viviana, I'm going to ask you something, and I hope you give me an honest answer," her mother said, looking her dead in the eye. "Are you and Felix involved in your late father's drug distribution?"

She looked at her mother in disbelief, although she knew exactly what her mother was thinking. Paula had caught her completely off guard, yet she knew she had to answer with a straight face if she wanted her mother to believe her.

"What? Are you serious, Mama?" Viviana responded as if she were totally taken aback and offended. "Of course not, Mama! Why would you even think that?" she questioned Paula, as her facial expression changed from surprised to baffled.

"Because when Linda called and asked had I seen Felix, she said people in the streets are saying Felix is pushing a lot of weight down here in Jersey," Paula said, repeating exactly what Felix's mother had told her.

"Well, Ma, you know Felix has always been a hustler, Viviana told her truthfully.

"I know, baby. I guess that's why Linda worries like she does. She don't want nothing bad to happen to that boy," her mother replied.

Viviana knew she had to tell Felix as soon as possible, but for now, she had to stick to the lie she had told, and the best way to do it was to change the subject. Paula knew her daughter well and Viviana knew it would only be a matter of time before the truth came out. And, if there was one thing Paula knew, it was the drug game, and she had learned it from one of the best hustlers who ever lived—her late husband, Ricardo Moreno.

Viviana looked at her mother and smiled, hoping it would ease her mother's mind. Then, she reached over and grabbed her hand gently.

"So, Mama, when are you gonna let me move you outta this place?" she asked, knowing the question would take the conversation in another direction.

"I'm fine right where I am, Viv. I got this place when your father passed and there's nobody here but me, so it suits me just fine."

"You could just move back into the Estate where you and daddy lived for years," Viviana suggested.

"I can't Viviana," Paula replied. Sadness resonated in her voice as she looked away with tears in her eyes. "Me and your father shared too much there, and the many memories still linger. I just couldn't take going back to live there," she said somberly. But I do make sure I go there every so often to check on the place."

"I know how you feel, Mama. I miss him too," Viviana told her, as she rubbed her mother's shoulder softly. "But, please, Mama, at least let me buy you something better than this."

"What's wrong with my place, Viv?" Her mother turned to face her.

"Nothin', Mama. I just want you to live like you lived when daddy was alive."

"Baby, you have your own life to live, so let mama live hers, okay?"

"Okay, Mama, but whatever you need you let me know."

"Okay, baby, I will." Paula smiled and leaned in to kiss her daughter on the cheek.

"I mean it, Ma … anything you need, you call me," she said, standing up from the sofa. "I gotta go now so I can go get ready for my trip to Colombia."

She gave her mother another hug and reminded her again to call if she ever needed anything.

"I'm fine, Viv. Your father left us both well off," Paula said, as Viviana opened the front door to leave.

They waved good-bye to one another and Viviana got inside her car. "Bye, Mama, talk to you later!" she yelled out from the window, before driving off.

As soon as Viviana was sure she was out of her mother's sight, she pulled out her iPhone to speed-dial her cousin, Felix. His phone went to voicemail and rather than leave a message, she hung up and redialed again.

"Come on, Felix, answer," she mumbled aloud, but to no avail.

By the time she had made it home, she had called Felix's phone five times back to back. She pulled her Bentley into her parking garage and turned off the ignition. By now, she was feeling anxious and aggravated, but she knew she had to talk to Felix ASAP. Once she was inside the house, she called again, and finally she got an answer.

"Hello," Felix's deep baritone answered.

"Hello? Felix I been blowin' your damn phone up! Wake yo' ass up," she shouted. "We need to talk!"

"What's up, Viv? Is somethin' wrong?" he wanted to know.

"I'm just gettin' home from goin' to see mama and—

"Oh, word, Felix said, cutting her off in midsentence. "So, how Aunt Paula doin'?" he asked.

"She good. . . she still won't let me move her out that damn town-house though," she answered.

Felix laughed because he knew how stubborn his aunt could be sometimes. "Damn, that's Aunt Paula for you," he said, followed by a chuckle. "But what's good, Cuz?"

"Well," Viviana began, "when me and mama was talkin', she told me Aunt Linda had been callin' her askin' her had she seen you."

"What?" Felix blurted out.

"Yeah, Felix, and that's not all," Viviana told him.

Now, Felix was curious. It didn't make sense that his mother would call his Aunt Paula asking about him, especially when she could have called him herself. He had been lying down in bed when Viviana first called him but hearing that his mother was calling around asking questions about him, caused him to sit straight up.

"Aunt Linda told mama that word on the streets is, you pushin' major weight."

"You bullshittin'!" Felix replied in an exasperated tone of voice. He sighed heavily and rubbed his hand across the top of his head. "Fuck, man!" He snapped angrily. "I tell you what, Viv, let me get up and put some clothes on, and then I'ma pull up on you."

"Alright, Felix. I'll be here," Viviana answered.

"Bet, Cuz, see you then," Felix said, before disconnecting the call.

Felix pulled up to Viviana's house in his cocaine-white Porsche truck, with all white interior. He walked up to her door and rang the doorbell. She opened the door dressed in a pink Manolo velour jogging suit, wearing pink Hello Kitty slippers on her feet.

"Hey, what's up, Felix," Viviana said, as she stepped to the side, allowing her cousin to enter.

"What's up, Cuz," he replied. He leaned in and gave Viviana a hug.

Of course, Felix had been to his cousin's home plenty of times, so leading the way, he headed to her massive all white living room, with Viviana following behind him.

"Cuz, you got this shit laid to the max," Felix said, just as he'd said many times before.

"You know how I do it. Ain't never no half-steppin' wit' me," she replied with a wide grin.

"That way!" Felix said, raising his hand in the air to give Viviana a high-five. They both laughed out loud.

Viviana took a seat in her favorite spot on the sofa, next to Felix, and handed him a container filled with weed. "Roll-up," she said.

"Shit, you ain't said nothin' but a word," he said, as he gutted the Philly and filled it with the weed.

"Now what's this shit about mama tellin' Aunt Paula she heard I'm pushin' major weight on the streets?" he asked seriously, as he hit the blunt and held the smoke before blowing it out.

"Yeah, Felix you might need to go on the block to see who runnin' their mouth and check them niggas," Viviana said in a tone that let him know she meant business.

Felix shook his head in agreement and took another toke of the blunt, before passing it to Viviana. "I got it covered, Cuz," he assured her.

"I hope so. 'Cause all I'm sayin' is, I know people gonna talk but shit. . . . Shit shouldn't be out there like that. . . . I mean, what the fuck goin' on, Felix?" she said, staring at her cousin intensely. She hit the blunt again and inhaled deeply, then she exhaled and released a stream of smoke from her nose. "I mean, you and me both know you the only one sellin' it on the streets and the only one people buyin' weight from. So, somebody talkin'. . . and you need to find out who it is, and *fast*," she added with a stern look glued on her face.

Felix looked off silently as if he was deep in thought, and then he reached in his pocket and pulled out his cell phone; however, after pressing a few numbers on the phone's keypad, he put the phone right back in his pocket. Viviana didn't bother to question him because she figured he'd started to make a call but changed his mind for whatever reason. Again, she hit the blunt and passed it back to Felix.

"So, here's the deal," she explained, "you gotta go talk to your boys and find out who's talkin' 'cause—"

"Say no more, Cuz," Felix interrupted, "I'm already on it, baby girl."

"Alright, make sure you handle that," she reiterated. "Oh, and I forgot to tell you, in a few days, I'ma be goin' to Colombia to see my aunt on my father's side of the family," she informed him.

With heavy eyes, Felix laid back on the sofa. "Oh yeah," he replied, "that's what's up."

"Yeah, I'ma go catch up, see how she doin' and what not… you know, surprise her." Viviana smiled.

"So, you goin' by yourself?" Felix asked.

"Yeah, it'll only be for a few days," she answered.

"Well, you be careful, Viv," he told his cousin sincerely.

"I will, Felix." She slumped back on the sofa next to him, with a childish grin on her face. "I'm high as hell," she added.

"Sheeit, me too, Cuz," he laughed. "But, damn, I'm still trippin' off that shit mama told Aunt Paula," he said in a serious tone. He held his hand up to his face and rubbed his chin. Who in the fuck out there runnin' their trap," he wondered aloud.

Viviana stood up and walked over to her bar to fix her and Felix a drink. "Yeah, I'm wonderin' the same damn thing," she said as she looked back over her shoulder towards him. "I know one damn thing. . . whoever it is gotta be checked, and real quick-like," she said.

"Cuz, don't even worry 'bout it. I told you I'm on it," Felix reminded her. As a matter of fact, I texted my boy Tony and he wanna meet up tomorrow," he told her. "That's what I was doin' when you saw me take my phone out earlier," he said.

Viviana walked back over to the sofa carrying two glasses. She handed Felix the glass of cognac, and she took a sip of the Pink Allure Moscato she had poured for herself.

"So what time y'all meetin' up?" she inquired.

"'Bout 4 o'clock. But listen, Cuz, we gonna handle that, just trust me," he assured her once again.

"Okay, just let me know what you find out," she replied, "'cause I can't have nobody puttin' my father's Empire in jeopardy. And be careful out there, Felix. But this shit gotta stop," she said, blowing weed smoke through her nose.

"Oh, fa'sho, Cuz. I'ma have this problem solved real quick."

He finished his drink, and he and Viv said their goodbyes.

CHAPTER 3

It was 3:45 p.m. the following day and Viviana was lying in bed watching *The Game Ain't 4 For Everybody*. Her phone rang, and she reached over to answer it.

"Hello," she said, greeting the caller.

"What's up, girl," Felix responded. "I was just hittin' you up to let you know I'm about to make that move to meet up with my man Tony.

"Oh, OK. Go handle that, Cuz," Viviana replied. "I was just layin' here watchin' a movie. I'm glad you called though 'cause I need to be up packin'," she said. "You know my flight leaves tonight around 7 o'clock," she reminded him.

"Fa'sho, I figured I'd call and let you know the deal, Cuz…you know, give you the 411 on where I'ma be at, 'cause you never know," he paused and continued, "niggas can be shady out here, but you already know that."

"Yeah, you right, Felix, just be careful, cuz."

"I will, Viv. But, check it, we meetin' up at the Sand Bar," he informed her.

"You mean the one in Jersey City?" she asked.

"Yeah, that one," he told her.

"OK. Cool. I know exactly where that's at," Viviana said.

"A'ight, Cuz," Felix said. "I'm pullin' up there now, so I'll hit you up later on," he said. "One." He pressed the call button and ended the call.

Felix pulled up to the Sand Bar in his candy-apple red Hummer, dressed in Gucci from head to toe, and the diamonds from his iced-out Presidential Rolex watch were blinding. After finding a parking spot, he sat in his truck and waited for Tony to arrive.

After about 15 minutes of waiting, he begin to get impatient. *Where this nigga at…*he thought to himself, as he held up his wrist to check the time on his watch. He pulled his phone back out of his pocket and dialed Tony's number.

"What's up, my nigga?" Felix asked when he heard Tony's voice on the other end. "Where you at?"

"I'll be there in 10 minutes," Tony stated. "You went in yet?" he questioned.

"Nah, man," Felix answered, "I'm still out in the parking lot waitin' on you."

"A'ight, bet. I'll be there in a few, man."

"A'ight, later," Felix replied and disconnected the call.

Not long after making the call to Tony, Felix noticed him pulling in the parking lot of the Sand Bar, where he sat waiting. He jumped out of his Hummer and flagged him down, so they could walk inside together.

Once the two of them had made it inside, they grabbed a couple of seats at a table and ordered a round of drinks.

"So, Tony… what's real, man?" Felix began. "Me and my folks been hearin' some things." Tony listened intently as he sipped on his Cognac and he could hear the frustration in Felix's voice. "Yeah, man word on the streets is, I'm pushing major keys out there," he elaborated.

"I know, man. . . . Dudes is talkin'," Tony said, confirming Felix's and Viv's suspicion. "I heard the same shit, yo'," he further explained. "That's why I'm glad we havin' this little sit-down. 'Cause on the real, I'm tryna figure things out just like you and your peoples, man."

Felix shook his head up and down as he listened to what Tony was telling him. When Tony finished talking Felix leaned in toward him and said in a low tone, as not to be overheard, "Man, I'ma need you to go chill on the block and keep a close eye out on what's goin' on out there… See if you can get me some answers and get back at me, dawg."

"Fa'sho, my nigga, you got it," Tony affirmed. "Don't even sweat it, consider it done," he added, as they stood up from the table and both gulped down the last of their drink.

Giving one another dap, they headed toward the door of the Sand Bar restaurant and made their exit.

"Yo', holla at me," Felix shouted over his shoulder, as he and Tony went their separate ways, walking towards their vehicle.

———————

It was 7:45 p.m. and Viviana was at the Atlantic City International Airport, and she had just boarded the plane for her flight to Colombia. She walked through the aisle in search of her seat that was located in the first-class section of the plane. After finding it, she proceeded to place her bag on the overhead designated for carry-on. As she sat down and got comfortable in her seat, her phone rang.

"Hello," she answered on the first ring.

"What's up, Viv?" Felix's voice belted out on the other end.

"Oh, hey, what's up Felix?"

"I was calling to make sure you made your flight on time," he told her.

"Yeah, I made it, so I'm good," she replied. "I just got to my seat and put my carry-on bag in the overhead compartment," she informed him.

"Okay, cool. But look, I had that lil' chat wit' my boy, Tony, and I got him hangin' out on the block to check things out," he explained. "I'll hit you up in a couple of days, after I hear somethin'."

"Alright," Viviana replied." She sat back in her seat and put her seatbelt on. "I gotta go now Felix because the plane is about to take off. My flight is scheduled to land in five hours and I'll give you a call once I've settled in," she added.

"That's cool, Cuz. I'll holla at you later tonight," he said. "Be safe, Viv," he told her, before ending the call.

━━━━━━━━

It was 1:45 a.m. and Viviana's flight had just landed at the Olaya Herrera Airport in Medellin, Colombia. After getting off the plane, she realized she'd neglected to arrange to have a car waiting for her, so she grabbed her luggage and headed out to one of the Ubers parked in front of the airport.

Thirty minutes later, she arrived at the upscale, 5-star Casa Pestagua Hotel Boutique and Spa, located inside the walls of Cartagena. The scenery outside the hotel was something right out of a fairytale. There was a huge courtyard with beautiful greenery everywhere and a light breeze filled the air. An outdoor pool with the prettiest blue water she'd ever seen seemed to mesmerize her at first sight. And, although it was dark out, the lighting around the hotel allowed her eyes a glimpse of its luxurious beauty.

After checking in at the front desk, she made her way to her room. She scanned her room key in the door and stepped into the spacious living quarters of the hotel. The décor of the room was laid out with antique furnishings, and the California King seemed to call out to her tired body. The minibar was fully stocked with bottled water and a variety of liquors. Right on top of the minibar was an ice-bucket filled with ice and a bottle of the hotel's most expensive wine, which room service had left prior to her arrival.

"Wow, this is beautiful," she said out loud as she looked around the private suite. *Peace and quiet... just what I need*, she thought.

She threw her bags across the bed and took her shoes off, before unpacking. The feel of the thick carpet beneath her feet was a much-needed relief from the 5-inch stilettos she'd been wearing all day. When she was finally done making herself at home, she laid out some comfortable clothing to change in after her shower.

Just as she begin to undress, her phone rang. *Now who could be phoning me already?* she thought as she released an annoyed sigh. She picked up the phone, looked at the screen, and the name on it read 'Felix'.

"What's up," she answered.

"You made it, Cuz?" Felix asked.

"Yeah, I'm finally here. Actually, I was about to take a shower right before you called..."

"A'ight, Viv. I'ma let you go handle that. I just wanted to see if your flight had landed safely," he said.

"Yeah, Felix, I'm good, but I'll call you later on after I get up."

"Holla at me then," he told her, before disconnecting the lines.

Viviana walked to the bathroom and turned the shower on before stepping inside. She was so exhausted, and she hadn't had a good night's sleep in a while.

The jet stream of the hot water hitting her tired body felt like heaven on earth. She stood underneath the water until the entire bathroom had filled up with steam and she could no longer see.

Once she felt clean and somewhat rejuvenated, she stepped out, and dried off with one of the hotel's big fluffy soft cotton towels.

After she'd lotion up her body really well, she made her way over to the minibar and filled one of the glasses with the complimentary wine that had been chilling on ice.

She climbed in bed, grabbed the remote and turned on the TV. However, after just a few sips, Viviana was fast asleep.

12:00 p.m.

Viviana hadn't realized just how tired she really was until she had woken up and noticed she'd slept until noon. She got up, walked over to her balcony, and looked out at the beautiful view of the city. The sun shined brightly, and the view was breathtaking! *I love it here,* she thought as her eyes scanned the city beneath her.

Still feeling fatigued, she went back inside and sat down on the bed. Grabbing the remote, she turned on the TV and decided to watch the news.

As she changed the channel from one to another in search of the news, she suddenly remembered she hadn't called her Aunt Maria to let her know she was in town. Her phone battery had been nearly dead when she had first arrived, so she had placed it on the charger and had planned to call her aunt after her shower, but instead, she'd fallen asleep.

So, she reached over and took the phone off the charger and dialed her Aunt's number.

Maria answered on the second ring. "¡Hola!" she said in her native tongue, which translates to *hello* in English.

"¡Hola! ¿Cómo está, Aunt Maria?" Viviana replied saying *hello, how are you?*

"Muy bien, gracias," Maria answered. "I'm doing well, thank you," she repeated, this time in English. Because Maria was fluent in both English and Spanish, it was nothing unusual for her to switch back and forth when talking with her relatives from the states.

"Aunt Maria, I arrived in Colombia earlier this morning. My plane landed at 1:45 a.m.," Viviana explained.

"Oh, okay," Maria said. "I can't wait to see you," she told Viviana.

"I can't wait to see you either, Aunt Maria," Viviana replied sincerely. "I miss y'all so much! It's been two years since I last came to visit," she reminded her aunt.

"Two years?" Marie repeated surprisingly. "Man, how time flies!" she said.

"But, I think I'ma rest for the day and I'll be by to see you tomorrow," Viviana told her. "Is that okay with you, Aunt Maria?"

"Of course, my dear niece," she answered with a smile. She could hardly wait to see her, and Viviana could hear the excitement in her voice. "Get some rest and I'll see you tomorrow, Viviana."

"OK, Aunt Maria. Talk to you tomorrow."

The following day Viviana left the hotel at 2 p.m. to go see her Aunt Maria. When Maria saw Viviana, she greeted her with a big hug and kissed her on both cheeks; she still couldn't believe it had been two years since they'd last seen one another.

The two of them sat outside on Maria's back porch and caught up on everything they'd been missing in each other's lives. Maria knew her niece's favorite alcoholic beverage was wine, so she had made sure to have a bottle.

"So, Viviana … tell me, si tú quieres (if you will) … how has my beautiful niece been doing in New Jersey?" she asked, in reference to Viviana. She noticed Viviana's hesitation to answer and she begin to rock back and forth in the lawn chair she was sitting in—her facial expression grew serious.

Viviana looked away as she sipped on her Merlot. She knew her aunt wouldn't receive her answer well, but she also knew she had to tell her. After a few more sips of wine, she took a deep breath and exhaled.

Turning her attention back towards her aunt she said, "Well … things are good for the most part, Aunt Maria … but somehow, the word has gotten out on the streets, and people are sayin' my cousin Felix, my mother's nephew, is pushin' kilos," she informed her.

"¡No puede ser!" she yelled out. "This can't be true, Viviana!". "We can't have that happening, Chica!" she said, shaking her head from side to side.

"I know … I know, Aunt Maria," Viviana agreed. She stopped sipping her Merlot and just held the glass in her hand. She continued staring at her aunt, hoping she could offer a solution to the problem.

"So, what you gonna do, Chica?" Maria inquired.

"Well, for starters, Felix has his boy Tony checkin' things out and he's gonna call me after he's heard something. But I made sure to tell him I'm not gonna jeopardize my father's Empire for *nobody*," she expressed with emphasis. Viviana paused to give Maria time to evaluate the information she'd just given her.

"Well, if he doesn't take care of it, we certainly will," Maria said in a stern tone.

A real true gangster, Maria was the person in charge of handling the front-end of Viviana's drug business. She stayed on top of making sure the kilos didn't come up short and ensured the product was distributed all over the country, from state to state. It would definitely start a war if the DEA or the FEDS ever found out that Viviana was *the* Belladonna moving all the drugs throughout the country—after all, she was the connect they had been searching for and she was definitely on their radar.

After a few moments of silence, Maria got up and walked over to the rose bush she had planted in the backyard. She appeared to be deep in thought as her fingers touched and rubbed the petals.

Noticing the far off look in her aunt's eyes, Viviana stood up from her lawn chair and walked over to where her Aunt stood and placed her hand on her shoulder.

"Aunt Maria," she said in soft tone, "I'm not worried about the DEA, FEDS, and nobody else, and I don't want you to worry either," she added.

Maria looked Viviana in her eyes and spoke. "I just have to keep you safe!" she told her niece. "I promised your father, my brother, I would. And I must honor my promise to him, Viviana," she said in her thick accent.

Viviana could see the sincerity in Maria's eyes when she mentioned her brother. The thought of him caused Viviana to look down in an effort to hide her sadness. She missed her father greatly and she would do whatever she had to do to keep his legacy alive.

"I hope Felix can take care of the problem," Maria said. "Because if the wrong people hear what's being said on the streets it could start a war, Viviana. Baby, you've got to be careful of the people we hold close to us, because sometimes, those could be the main ones trying to destroy us!" Maria turned and walked back toward the house to go inside, Viviana walked closely behind her.

"I know, Aunt Maria, but please try not to worry," Viviana replied as she followed her aunt through the house.

Maria went over to one of the closets and opened the door. "Here is all the money that has come in from the states down South," she said, pointing inside the closet at the neat stacks of money.

Maria had collected a total of a billion dollars from Viviana's drug distribution and she nearly filled the closet from top to bottom.

CHAPTER 4

A week later, back in the states…

At the clothing store, Viviana sat at her desk going through her computer. Wanting to be sure she had been crossing her T's and dotting her I's, she carefully checked all her recent files. Half way through, a knock came on the office door and it was Sharon.

"Yes, come on in!" she shouted.

"Hey, Viv," Sharon said upon entering, "customers are asking when we'll be getting some more Fendi shades and Fendi bags in…"

"Oh yeah? My mind has been so preoccupied these days, I forget to do things sometimes," she said, smiling.

"It's OK, I understand. But we definitely need to get more in as soon as possible, Viv," Sharon said, as she sat down at the desk with Viviana.

"Well, actually, you must have been reading my mind this morning," Viviana said, "because that's kind of what I'd planned to discuss with you today."

"OK, what we need to talk about?" Sharon asked. "Everything okay, ain't it?"

"Oh, yeah, everything is great," Viviana replied. "I was just gonna tell you we need to drive to the warehouse to go through the inventory that came in two weeks ago, that's all," she explained to her cousin. "And since you mentioned it, I'm sure the Fendi shades and bags came in with that order."

"Oh, okay. You know I'm ready whenever you are, so when we goin'?" Sharon asked.

"I think the sooner the better 'cause we missin' money if we don't have what the customers askin' for," Viviana said. "So, we can go once the store closes today, if you have time."

"Yeah, sure, Viv," Sharon agreed. "I don't have much to do when I get off anywa—"

"OK, then," Viviana quickly replied. "We need to go do that *today* then." She looked at Sharon and then turned her focus toward the window. Momentarily, she stood there quietly with a blank expression on her face as if her mind had gone to another place.

"Is something wrong, Viv?" Sharon asked. "What is it that you not tellin' me? You know you can tell me anything," Sharon said in a concerned tone.

Viviana continued to gaze out the window with a faraway look in her eyes, almost mysteriously.

"What is it, Viv?" Sharon repeated the question. "Talk to me, Cuz. . ."

"I don't know right now, Sharon," Viviana answered. "But something just doesn't feel right," she said, turning her focus back to Sharon. "I can't put my finger on it right now, but my gut never lies.

———

It was 10:00 p.m. and Viviana and Sharon were still at the warehouse bursting open the shipment packages, going through the inventory.

"OK, here we go, Sharon. I finally found the box with the shades," Viviana told Sharon, as she tore into the big box.

Sharon grabbed the box cutter to open another package and inside that one was the Fendi bags. "I got the Fendi bags right here, Viv," she said.

"OK, good. So, take these two boxes and set them over to the side so we can finish going through the rest of the shipment," Viviana told her.

Sharon took the boxes and placed them at the door near the entrance, where she and Viv had parked their vehicles. "Viv I'ma open up the other boxes over here," Sharon said, as she walked over to a different set of packages marked fragile.

"Well, before you go through them I should probably let you know that I'm looking for more than just the regular inventory," Viviana said.

"Oh, okay," Sharon replied, staring at her cousin knowingly. She knew how Viviana got down, so she had an idea of what else could be in the boxes. Now, it made sense as to why Viviana had been so anxious to get straight to the warehouse after work.

"Yeah, I had a few keys of coke shipped in and they should be in one of these boxes," Viviana said gesturing toward the many boxes stacked on the floor before them. "I've got some good connects on the outside of the postal department that look out for me 'cause being in the game, I gotta always make sure all my I's stay dotted and all my T's stay crossed."

"How many keys were supposed to come in?" Sharon asked curiously.

"At least 300," Viviana answered as if it were legal. There was so much coke in the warehouse, she would surely be put away for life if she were to get busted at that very moment; however, true to form, she was cool, calm, and collective. She had answered the question without batting an eye.

After ripping open a few more of the boxes, Sharon informed her they were all there, but the two of them did a recount just to be sure.

"Now that we're done we need to clean everything up, so we can get goin'," Viviana said. "I need you to take the kilo shipment to the spot and stash it. I'll get the rest of the boxes and keep them in my truck until I get to work tomorrow, and then we can put the new merchandise out for the customers," Viviana said.

"Well I'ma get on outta here and I'll call you later," Sharon said as she hugged Viviana.

"Be careful, Sharon, and make sure you call me as soon as you get the shipment delivered."

With her Glock 9-millimeter loaded and ready to blast a nigga, she watched as her cousin placed the keys of coke safely in her truck. Then, she locked up her warehouse and got in her Infinity truck and waited until she knew Sharon was in the clear. Once Sharon drove off, she sped off behind her.

It was almost 11:30 p.m. and by now, Viviana was beyond exhausted and all the unpacking at the warehouse had caused her to work up an appetite. So, she pulled out her cell phone and spoke into the receiver and asked Siri to order her a pizza.

Not long after, she pulled up to the Pizza Hut and double-parked, hoping she wouldn't get a ticket. Hopping out of the truck, she ran inside to pick up her order.

Thirty-minutes later, she had finally made it home and parked in her garage.

Felix ass ain't called me yet, she though, as she unlocked the door to her house. *What the hell is goin' on with this nigga... he shoulda' called me hours ago... something not right...*

Pushing the thought to the back of her mind, she went to her room to get comfortable. She grabbed her black lace robe by Roberto Cavalli from her closet and headed to the bathroom to shower away the stresses of the day.

Once she had showered and applied her favorite bedtime lotion, she decided to call Felix. "I wonder what the hell this nigga doin' so important that he can't pick up the damn phone," she mumbled, before taking a bite of pizza.

With a big sigh, she became more annoyed when she realized she had laid her phone down on the table in the kitchen and had to get back up to get it. "Damn, can a bitch get comfortable and rest!" she said out loud, as she stomped to the kitchen.

She grabbed her phone and quickly made her way back to the soft sofa and plopped herself down. She tapped the key to speed dial Felix and took a big gulp of berry blue Powerade while she waited for him to pick up.

"Hello," he said after the fourth ring.

"What's going on Felix?"

"Oh, what's up, Viv? I been meanin' to call you, but I got kinda tied up," he replied.

"Yeah, OK. I was wondering why you hadn't called," she said.

"My bad, Cuzzo. But on the real, I ain't heard nothin' back from Tony yet," he said.

"Damn. Really? Well, you was supposed to call me a week ago, Felix…." Viviana took the phone away from her ear and looked at it with the screw-face as if Felix could see her. "Come on now, Cuz," she said, "you ain't tryna play me, are you?" She shook her head from side to side because the words had slipped from her mouth before she could stop them.

"Hell nah, Cuz!" Felix answered in a defensive tone. "I can't believe you even askin' me some shit like that, Viv. You know I fucks wit' you the long way," he assured her. "For real though, I just been runnin' back and forth handlin' business, that's all," he repeated.

"I understand that, Felix, but yo' ass always on the go." She laughed. "But, anyway," she said as she inhaled and exhaled deeply, "let me know when you hear from him, okay? Oh, and yo' ass still coulda called to check on me... you ain't even call to see if I had made it back safely from Colombia," she added.

"You right again, Cuzzo. My bad... I'ma make it up to you though," he promised.

So, did you even call Tony to see what was going on Felix? "Of course, I did... he told me he ain't been on the block yet... you know how it is when you constantly runnin'. He said he would let me know somethin' as soon as he find somethin' out," Felix answered.

"Well, I guess I'ma just have to find out myself 'cause I told you I can't have my father's Empire—"

"Viv, I know dawg... it's just that we been busy, but it's gonna get done, trust me," he said, hoping he sounded convincing.

Viviana took another sip of her Powerade. "OK, Felix. Listen, I'm takin' you for your word, so don't let me down. As soon as you hear from that nigga, let me know! Alright?"

"I won't let you down, Cuz. That's my word. But look, I'ma get on off this phone and I'll hit you up later. Maybe we can go have some drinks or something on me," he said, in an attempt to get back in his cousin's good graces.

Viviana smiled and said, "Alright... I guess I can let you buy me a few drinks." They both laughed. "Well, let me go, Boo. I'll holla at you later," she said.

"A'ight, Viv, holla back," Felix replied, before hanging up. Viviana didn't miss how Felix contradicted himself by first saying he had not heard from Tony, then when the question came up again, he said he had talked to him. "Hmm, something's not adding up right." She thought as she hung up the phone.

The next night 1:00 a.m. South City Grille

Viviana and Felix sat at the bar buying drink after drink, getting fucked up, and the night appeared to be going well.

"So, Viv, how was Colombia?" Felix asked.

"It was good… did a lot of catchin' up with the family and checked on my Aunt Maria, you know, things like that," she answered before taking another sip of her drink.

"You should let me take that trip with you next time," Felix suggested.

Viviana looked at Felix with a smirk on her face. "Who you? You wanna go to Colombia?" she asked in a surprised tone. "I don't know about that now," she told him.

"Why not?" Felix replied.

"Well, for one thing, you way too busy to be tryna to take a trip to Colombia." Viviana's voice was filled with sarcasm.

Felix thought nothing of the remark she had just made and took another sip of his drink. "Yeah, you probably right, Viv," he agreed without further debate.

Viviana didn't bother responding; instead, she bopped her head to the music, looking sexy in the black Cavalli dress she'd worn.

Suddenly, a tall light skin dude came up to her at the bar. She looked at him and thought, *damn, dude is sexy and bold as hell!* He was dressed in a pair of black Represent jeans with a black Kings thermal, both by Rocawear, and he wore a pair of all black Air Yezzy shoes on his feet.

He walked over to the bar and stood next to her.

"Hello, Ms. Lady. What's your name?" he asked politely.

Viviana looked up and noticed how tall and just how handsome he really was. The diamonds on his watch and bracelet nearly blinded her.

"Viviana," she said, as she extended her hand out to his, "and yours?"

"I'm Giovanni. Nice to meet you, Viviana," he replied. He took her hand and kissed it softly.

She looked at him flirtatiously and smiled. "Oh, excuse my manners, but this is my cousin Felix, but I assume you knew he was related to me, since you were bold enough to come over here and ask me my name." she said gesturing her head in Felix's direction.

Felix reached over, and he and Giovanni shook hands.

"Well, as beautiful as you are, I figured you were worth a beat-down. Can I steal you for a few minutes?" Giovanni asked, gently tugging her by the arm.

"Why sure," she said. "I'll be right back, Felix," she told him.

"A'ight, Cuzzo. I'll be right here."

Viviana got up from the bar and followed Giovanni to a table on the other end of the bar.

"So, Viviana… where did you get that beautiful name from?" Giovanni asked.

"Well, it's a Colombian name," she said.

"Oh, I see… that makes sense. So, are both your parents Colombians?"

"Only my father," she answered. "My mother is American, but he met my mother here in New Jersey, and they moved to Colombia together, and that's when they had me," she smiled bashfully. Giovanni returned the smile.

"Why you lookin' at me like that, Giovanni?"

"Because you're so beautiful," he answered honestly. For a brief moment, he looked down as if her beauty was just too much to take in, and just as quickly, he turned his gaze back toward her.

"Thank you, Giovanni, that's so sweet," she laughed softly. "So-um, where is your lady? I know a handsome man like you has to be taken," she said.

"Well, I stay too busy to have one… honestly, my life is mad crazy sometimes," he admitted.

"So. . . you sayin' you a hustler?" Viviana blurted out.

Giovanni was somewhat taken aback, and the expression on his face said as much.

"What made you ask me that?" he questioned her curiously.

"Mmm," she said, licking her lips like a hungry lioness, "I love the way you say my name, Giovanni. But the only reason I asked you that is because I know a hustler when I see one." She smiled and winked her right eye at him.

"Oh yeah? Is that right?" he asked, with a crooked grin on his face. "Well, Viviana… I-um- I guess you could say… I'm a business man in the pharmaceutical business.

"Oh… okay…" she said, liking the sound of his answer, "I *love* a black man that handles his business," she told him in a seductive tone. She smiled at him deviously.

"Now you tell me, Viviana… what do you do for a living? If you don't mind me asking," he added.

Viviana burst out with a loud laugh. "Funny you would ask that," she said. "Truth is, I *also* have an eye for business…"

"Um-hm," Giovanni replied. "You don't say… "And just what type of business might you have an eye for?"

"I own a clothing store located in the mall, and also a deli on the Southside of New Jersey." Now it was Giovanni's turn to smile at what he was hearing.

"Wow, Viviana! You're a business woman for real, huh?"

"Yes, I am, and you think your life is hectic?" She laughed again. "I definitely know the feeling," she said.

"When do you have time for yourself, Viviana?" Giovanni wanted to know.

"Really, Giovanni? Come on now… I know you know how it is… to be honest, I really don't. I mean, I'm constantly tied up in meetings for one thing or another. But I can honestly say I love my life," she said truthfully.

"I can understand that, Ms. Lady," he said genuinely.

Giovanni was a true boss, and a boss of his stature didn't have time to worry about sleep or rest—not as long as there was money to be made. A man like him often kept a low profile so it must have been fate that caused he and Viviana to cross paths tonight. With so many niggas gunning for his position in the streets, he rarely frequented bars, or clubs for that matter.

"I got an idea," he said, as if a light bulb had just came on in his head, "why don't you let me take you out sometimes to take away some of that stress?"

"You would do that, Giovanni?" Viviana asked in a shy voice.

"Hell, yeah! I'm feelin' you real hard right now and I just wanna take you out and show you a good time," he said, rubbing his hand ever so lightly across her cheek.

The touch of his hand on her skin felt so good she thought she'd melt—especially since it had been a while since she'd been with a man.

"Ooh… You betta stop that," she said as she looked at Giovanni with lust-filled eyes."

"Stop what? Did I do something wrong?" he asked. He quickly pulled his hand back, thinking maybe he'd crossed the line.

"No-no-not at all… it's just that the warmth of your hand against my skin felt sooo good," she cooed honestly.

"Well what would you do if I kissed you?" he asked her.

"Well, I don't think you should do that… at least, not here," she told him.

"Why? I won't hurt you, Ms. Lady," he assured her.

"Oh, I'm not worried about that," she quickly told him, "I just don't want to end up in your bed later."

The mere thought of Viviana's last statement caused Giovanni to reach his hands out and place one on each side of her face. Gently, he pulled her face toward his and kissed her softly, yet deeply.

"Mmm . . ." She moaned as she allowed their tongues to do the French tango. Remembering where they were, she pulled her face away from him. "Giovanni, you have to stop before I end up leaving with you."

"Well, let's go then," he suggested with a smile.

"Are you serious?" She laughed. "I was just kidding," she said only half telling the truth.

"I'm very serious," he replied. He leaned over and placed a soft kiss on her lips and whispered, "Come on, baby… let's get outta here… come spend the night with me, Viviana."

"Giovanni, really? I'm not that kind of girl," she told him in a more serious tone. "I mean… you are one of the most sexy and attractive men I've come across in a long time, but that's just not how I get down."

The two sat in silence as they looked at one another eye to eye. Then, Giovanni reached his hand across the table and grabbed Viviana's hand inside his own. He cleared his throat before speaking and chose his words carefully.

"Viviana, I hope I haven't offended you in any way 'cause that's the last thing I wanna do. I wasn't in any way suggesting that you're one of those loose women who doesn't demand respect," he told her, as he rubbed her hand gently with his thumb.

"I can tell from our conversation and just from the little bit you've told me about yourself that you've got a good head on your shoulder. You're the type of woman who demands respect just by entering a room, and baby, I wouldn't have it any other way," he said.

"I said it before and I'll say it a million times more if I have to, I'm really feelin' you. The conversation is amazing, and I just wanna get to know you better on a more personal level. "You just might be the future Mrs. Giovanni," he said jokingly. "One never knows where he might find love." His tone was deep, serious; he held Viviana's gaze as if he were casting a spell on her.

"What are you saying, Giovanni? You don't even know me."

"I know, but I want to get to know you. So, what's it gonna be?" He reached underneath the table and rubbed her thigh. "It's like this, you don't have a man, I don't have a woman, and we are both grown consenting adults," he said. "We both know we're feeling each other, so why not give it a try and make it exclusive, baby?"

Viviana smiled and replied, "Okay, fine, but first let me go tell my cousin I'm leaving."

"Cool, but you never answered my question… will you be my lady?"

Just as she was about to get up from the table, she looked over at Giovanni and smiled. "Yes, Giovanni… I would love to be your wife, I mean lady," and with that said, they both burst out laughing.

The two stood up from their seated positions and Viviana led the way over to the bar where Felix was sitting, and Giovanni walked closely behind her. Once she'd made it over to Felix, she tapped him on the shoulder to get his attention.

"Felix," she said, speaking loudly over the music, "I just wanted to let you know I'm 'bout to bounce on up outta here with Giovanni!"

Felix turned his head and looked over his shoulder at her as if she was speaking a foreign language. He couldn't believe what he was hearing. It was very unlike Viviana to trust strangers, especially being in the business she was in.

"Hold on, Cuz… you kiddin' me, right?" Felix said. "Viv, you just met dude," he said, attempting to whisper in her ear.

"Yeah, and so what nigga?" She laughed and added, "I'm grown!"

Felix turned his attention towards Giovanni and gave him a look that said: *'you better take care of her'* and he shook his head from side to side. Viviana leaned down and kissed her cousin on his cheek and grabbed Giovanni by the hand.

The two headed to the exit of the bar and before Viviana left out, she turned around and gave Felix a cute little wave.

That damn girl, he thought to himself, as he smiled and waved back. And, just like that, Viviana was gone with her new-found friend, Giovanni.

2:30 a.m. At the Wilshire Grand Hotel

As Viviana crawled on top of Giovanni, he grabbed her by her waist and pulled her closer to him. The way he kissed her softly, caused her to moan.

"Aaah, mmmh… Make love to me, Giovanni," she begged in quiet whispers.

"You ready for that," he asked in a husky voice. He looked her deeply in the eyes as if he could see straight through to her soul.

"Yes, baby, I'm ready," she cooed, "I want you so bad, Giovanni," she told him.

He turned her on her back and began to plant soft, gentle kisses up and down her body. When his lips brushed against her stomach, she almost lost it. She moved her head from side to side and her breath nearly caught in her throat. She could hardly take the anticipation of what would come next.

He scooted down further and used his hands to gently push her legs apart; Viviana began panting in short breaths like a woman who had just gone into labor. Wanting to take his time, Giovanni pulled her thong to the side and kissed her right on the opening of her honey well, before blowing on it lightly.

"Oh my God," she moaned, and grabbed his head tightly.

Giovanni was very skilled between the sheets and he definitely knew how to make love to a woman; however, he wanted to savor the moment. So, again, he kissed her wetness, and again, he blew on it lightly, causing her to spread her legs even wider.

"I'ma need you to come on up outta these," he groaned, lightly tugging at her thongs. Slowly, he pulled them down her legs and then threw them on the floor.

Without warning, he dove his head between her legs and began licking her pussy lips, as if it were the best thing he'd ever tasted. He stuck his tongue as deeply inside her as he possibly could. And, with skilled precision, he rotated back and forth, sucking her clit, and licking her hole. She grabbed him again by the sides of his head and held his head firmly on her G-spot.

"Ooh, aaah, Giovanni-van, mmm… Giovanni, baby… don't stop," she begged in between moans. "My pussy is so wet… oh my God, it feels so good baby, mmm…"

"You like that, baby?" he managed to ask, briefly glancing at her.

"Yes, baby! It feels so good, mmm…"

Giovanni smiled, knowing he had made his mark.

When he began to lick faster and harder, Viviana's body began to tremble, and she could feel herself on the verge of an orgasm, and

"Ooh, ohh, right-th-th-there, baby! I'm about to cum… umm! Giovanni, baby…I'm about to cum all in your mouth, baby! Oh-my-Godddd!" she hollered out without shame. "I'm cummin', baby!" Her legs shook, and her head turned from side to side and she squeezed his head tightly. Then she grabbed the pillow next to her and dug her fingernails deeply into. When her moans grew louder, she wrapped both legs around his head and nearly screamed, "I'm cummin'! I'm cummin'!"

Giovanni sucked and licked like a famished animal lost in the wilderness, and he didn't plan to let one drop go to waste.

Viviana's breathing finally started to slow down as she lay there panting, breathlessly.

With that same soft touch, he kissed her on each thigh, making his way up to her stomach, and then kissed her breasts before gently sucking on her nipples.

Over the next hour, Giovanni pleasured Viviana without wanting anything in return. He had made her cum over and over again; her legs had become so weak, she doubted if she could even stand. He had been such a gentleman, and he had taken his time pleasing her.

Now they lay in bed, her with her head lying on his chest, and he, with his arms wrapped around her tightly. He kissed the top of her head as he held her close.

"Did you enjoy that, baby?" he asked her.

"Did I?" She laughed. "Yes, baby… you did that," she told him. "That was amazing," she said, as she leaned up to kiss his lips.

"Well, I'm happy you enjoyed it, baby… I just wanted you to relax and take some pressure off," he said truthfully. "But, just so you know, next time I'ma get some of that pussy." They both laughed.

"You so crazy," she said as she playfully punched him on the arm. "So, you never had intentions of fuckin' me?"

"Not at all. I never wanted sex from you. I just wanted to drive you crazy eatin' that sweet pussy." He smiled at Viviana, and she smiled back.

By now, she was lost in a lust-filled daze, and for now, she belonged to him, and in her mind, he belonged to her.

CHAPTER 5

A week later, Viviana went down to Chicago, Illinois, to purchase a loft style condo. Although she had no intentions of permanently moving, she had decided some time ago to invest in a nice little spot where she could get away from time to time. The loft was beautiful, and it was located in Winamac Lofts of Chicago.

She had known from the start that dealing drugs came with a price. She'd invested in the expensive hideaway, so she could check on the money she had coming in from state to state—a place where no one would think to look for her.

Later that day, she stood in her new loft looking out of the bay window. The movers had just buzzed to let her know they had arrived with her furniture.

"Hello, Ms. Moreno?" one of the movers called out.

"Yes," Viviana said, speaking through the intercom.

"We have a delivery for you, ma'am!"

"OK, great," she replied. "I'm buzzing you guys through now."

She made her way over to the front door and unlocked it to let them in so they could place her furniture.

———————

Later that evening after Viviana had hung all of her wall art, she took a seat on the sofa and poured herself a glass of Merlot. *Wow,* she thought to herself, as she looked around at the furniture in the loft… *I have great taste if I say so myself.*

After a few glasses of wine, she decided to take a hot soothing bubble bath in her Queen Ann tub. She rolled herself a nice fat blunt and thought, *one more glass of wine won't hurt.*

As she sat soaking in the tub, she sipped her Merlot and took a pull of the blunt, and just as she got comfortable her phone rang.

"Now who can this be?" she said in an irritated tone, "can't a girl just relax!" When she reached over and grabbed her phone, she realized it was Felix calling. "Hello," she said.

"What's up, Cuz?" came the voice on the other line.

"What's going on, Felix?" she asked.

"Just chillin'... you know," he replied.

"What's up though?" she asked again, as she took a deep pull from the blunt.

"So, where you at, Viv?" he asked.

"I'm down here in the Chi," she told him.

"Word? What's down there?"

"Just had to get away for a lil' bit, that's all," she answered.

"Yeah, I was about to say I haven't seen you in a few days," Felix said.

"Yeah, man, just down here handlin' a few things, but fuck that, enough about me," she said, changing the subject, "I wanna hear about *you*."

"Well, I talked with Tony and he said the word on the streets is I'm pushin' a lot of keys and—

"Nigga we already know that much," she snapped harshly.

"Yeah, but let me finish," he said continuing, "well, this dude that be buyin' a few ounces from me is the one who told people I was pushin' it like that... it's harmless though, dude straight."

"See… it's harmless to you but not me! How in the hell he know you got keys, Felix?" Viviana asked sarcastically.

"I guess he musta saw one of the keys when I cut the ounces off for him."

Viviana couldn't believe what she was hearing, and he shook her head from side to side as if she were baffled.

"Damn, Felix!" she said, raising her voice, "Like what the fuck was you thinkin', man? Why the fuck you didn't do that shit in the back room? I mean, what made you do that shit in front of him? Shit man! Now see yo' ass was tryna flex and that flexin' shit could get yo' ass killed, man! What the fuck?"

Felix felt like a complete asshole and he knew he had pissed his cousin off big time. At a loss for words, he held the phone in silence. Knowing he had to come up with a good explanation, he thought carefully before finding his voice to speak again.

"Viv, Cuz, I know I fucked that up," he began, "and nothin' I say can change that," he said somberly. "Yo', word, I fucked up!"

"Felix, damn! I can't even believe yo' ass didn't already have the shit bagged up! The only thing that nigga shoulda seen was the damn scale when you was weighin' his shit up!" she said, her tone frustrated.

"You, right, Cuz," was all he could say.

"Felix, I'ma get off this phone but you and me gonna have to talk about this shit face to face; I'll be back in a few days, so we can meet up then," she told him.

"A'ight, Viv, my bad dawg."

"Damn right, yo' bad! That nigga can come back anytime, set you up and kill yo' ass!"

Again, Felix was at a loss for words and said nothing. After a few moments of awkward silence, he finally said, "I'll holla at you when you get back, Cuz."

"You sure will Viviana snapped," and disconnected the line without so much as a simple goodbye.

Felix looked at his phone. *Damn, I fucked up* he thought. He, better than anyone, knew how private his cousin was. She didn't take to people all up in her business. After all, it *was* *her* business. Realizing he could've possibly messed everything up, deep down inside he couldn't blame her for being mad at him. "Fuck!" he yelled.

———

Early one morning on the south side of New Jersey, Viviana walked through the back door of the Deli that she owned.

"Martha! Gloria!"

"¡Hola, mami," Martha said as she kissed Viviana on the cheek.

"¡Hola!" Gloria greeted.

Viviana grabbed an apron and the three women walked to the front to get prepared for the day.

"So, ladies, I know I don't get out this way often, but because I trust you both, I know everything is under control," Viviana said.

"Of course, Viv, we always make sure everything is handled the right way," Gloria said.

Martha was the oldest of the two sisters, and also the one who handled the business part of the Deli. Gloria, on the other hand, handled the security part of the Deli, and everyone knew she was no joke—definitely not one to be messed with!

Martha looked at Viviana and smiled happily. "So, Cuzzie, how have things been going your way?"

Viviana hesitated before answering. She didn't want to worry the women, but she was so angry at the stupid shit Felix had done, she really needed to vent. She sighed heavily and began to explain the conversation she'd previously had with him.

"Well, Martha, Gloria, you will never believe what my cousin Felix did! You've both heard me mention him before, right? Well, anyway, he's my cousin on my mother's side of the family," she reminded them.

The two ladies were all ears, and both stood quietly wanting to hear everything Viviana had to share with them. They loved Viviana as if she were their own little sister and because of that, they were very protective of her.

"Tell us, Viv," Martha said.

"Yes, what happened," Gloria asked.

"For the most part, things have been going pretty smooth, like always, and the money is still comin' in," Viviana told them, looking from one to the other. "But recently," she continued, "I found out Felix slipped up and let a muthafucka find out he had a key in the damn trap house where he handles the business at."

The mere thought of Felix's stupidity caused a frown to spread across her face and she still couldn't believe her right-hand could be so careless.

Martha and Gloria looked at one another then back at their niece, neither saying a word.

"He said dude went over there to get a few ounces, and instead of him handling business in private, his dumb ass cut the shit off the brick right in front of the nigga." Viviana was livid, and she let it be known.

Gloria could hardly wait to get her two-cents in and Felix had better be lucky he was nowhere around at the moment; otherwise, she would've probably chewed him a new asshole. "Why the hell didn't he have the shit already bagged up?" she said louder than she intended—good thing they were the only ones in the deli.

"Exactly!" Viviana agreed. "That's the same damn thing I asked *his* ass!"

In disbelief, Martha and Gloria shook their heads from side to side, almost simultaneously.

"You right, Viv, that fool slippin' for re—

"Viviana, you my cousin and I love you dearly," Gloria said, cutting Martha off midsentence, "and you don't need nobody puttin' you in jeopardy of being possibly set up by the DEA! And you damn sure don't need them nosy ass FEDS comin' around askin' a lot of fuckin' questions!" she said, "'cause once they show up, you know it's a problem!" she added.

"I don't think that's gonna happen, Gloria," Viviana said, "at least I sure as hell hope not." Each one looked at the other, all three wearing a serious facial expression. "I'ma tell his ass how serious this is when I see him, but I'm sure he already knows that. And, I hate to cut him off, 'cause he brings in hella profits," she explained, "but cousin or no cousin we can't do business that way! I'ma give his ass another chance though 'cause he been down so long... and in this game, it's wiser to keep him than to let him go... at least for now," she said.

"Yeah, you got a point," Martha said, "and what's even more important is the fact that this is our late uncle's Empire we tryna keep alive. And no one is gonna destroy it, period!"

The room fell silent while each woman stood in her own thoughts. After a few minutes Viviana spoke. "When I get back across town I'm gonna have a heart to heart with him and I'ma let him know there can be *no more fuck-ups* or he's out!"

"You tell him that shit too, Cuzzie," Gloria snapped. "I know he don't want no problems 'cause the nigga might be yo' family but he ain't mine," she said as she walked away from the counter to unlock the doors for the customers.

"Okay, team enough of that, let's get ready to make some sandwiches!" Viviana popped both of her cousins on the butt playfully and they all laughed.

As Viviana walked off, her mind was still heavy on Felix. *Lord, for his sake, I hope he's being truthful to me and loyal to this Empire... 'cause only God can save him from my family's wrath if I find out he's been deceitful in any kind of way...*

Not long after the doors of the deli had been opened, the customers started pouring in. People of all nationalities stopped in to grab breakfast or lunch; some were usual customers, and from time to time, a few new faces would stop by to patronize the deli.

The day seemed to fly by, but still, both Gloria and Martha were glad to have had the extra help from Viviana because they had stayed busy all day.

When things finally slowed down the three were happy to take a break.

"Whew-wee, the customers were coming in like crazy today," Gloria said, as they grabbed a seat at one of the tables.

"But, on another note, I met this flyy-ass gentleman at the South City Grille down the street on the Southside," Viviana said. A slight smile begin to spread across her face as she recalled her night with Giovanni.

"I heard that place is nice and has really good food," Gloria said.

"Yes, it's really nice," Viviana agreed. "Felix and I had gone there to discuss business and have a few drinks."

Seemingly confused, Martha scrunched up her face and said, "I thought you said you met a guy? So, you went with Felix?"

Viviana couldn't help but laugh because although her cousins were very business oriented, they were both still just as hood. They loved to gossip, and both were nosy as hell.

"If you would stop asking questions and let me tell the story you would know what happened," she said, causing all three ladies to laugh out. "Anyway, as I was saying, *Martha,*" she emphasized jokingly, "this sexy-ass guy walked over to the bar where we were sitting, and he approached me. . . dude was iced-out. He was a light-skin, tall, sexy muthafucka. . . . No lie, I wanted to fuck him right then and there!"

By now, Both Martha and Gloria were all ears as they anticipated all the good tea that was about to be spilled.

"So, he comes up to me and right away, I was dazed by his fineness. I mean, the way he stepped to me caught me by surprise, he did the shit so smooth and suave. The nigga had charm and appeal," she said, fanning herself as if she were suddenly hot; her animation made them burst out into a fit of laughter.

"So, what happened next?" Gloria asked.

"Well, he asked me my name, and after I told him, he invited me to sit with him at a table, and the rest is history," she said, knowing this would get a reaction from her cousins.

"Come on, Viv, you can't leave us hanging!" said Martha.

"At least tell us his name," Gloria probed.

"His name is Giovanni," she said. She couldn't believe this guy she'd just met had her seriously blushing. She smiled as she continued, "At the table, he grabbed my hand and kissed it, in true gentleman fashion. We talked for the rest of the night and got to know one another." Viviana winked devilishly.

"Oh no you didn't!" Martha blurted out. "You gave him some, didn't you!"

"A lady never tells," she said, smiling so big her face hurt. "But, what I will tell you is I think I may have found someone to add what's been missing in my life."

"And what's that?" Gloria asked.

"The dick!" Martha answered, and they high-fived one another, laughing hysterically.

"Girl, girl, girl," Viviana replied. "The man is blessed and packing!"

"I'm happy you found somebody, Cuzzie!"

"Me too," Martha concurred. "I hope he's the one 'cause you deserve a good man."

"Thanks y'all. I could sit here and talk about that man all day," she blushed, "but I gotta get going now. I'll holla next time I'm on this end," Viviana said, as she leaned over and gave both women a quick hug and a kiss on the cheek.

"Let us know when you and Mr. Lover Man set the date for the wedding," Martha teased. Again, they burst out laughing.

"And make damn sure you get things straight with that damn Felix!" Gloria told her, 'cause we gotta keep this Empire strong and we don't need no mishaps. Uncle Ricardo would turn over in his grave if anything ever happened to something he grinded so hard to keep alive."

"I know you guys," Viviana replied, now in a more serious tone. "I stand strong in my father's wish and I will never let him down," she said sincerely, as she made her exit through the back door of the Deli. "Y'all hold it down now!" she shouted after she had made it to her car.

Gloria pulled out her pump shotgun and held it up high in the air. "We got this, Cuzzie, no worries!"

Viviana smiled and hopped inside of her Mercedes Benz 350, pumped the music, and sped off like the boss bitch she knew she was.

CHAPTER 6

The following Saturday as Viviana lay on her sofa watching Scarface, her phone rang. She reached over to pick it up off the glass marble table and realized it was Giovanni. With a huge smile she answered.

"Hello," she said trying hard to hide her excitement.

"Hello, beautiful," Giovanni's sexy voice replied, "how you been stranger?"

"I been good and you, my sexy friend," she said, as she blushed on the other end.

Shirtless, and wearing a pair of Gucci jeans, with his Gucci slides dangling on his feet, Giovanni smiled and got comfortable on his black leather sofa.

"I've been doing good as well, just busy as usual, but you of all people know about that life," he said, rubbing his hand across his head.

"Yes, I definitely understand that life can be very busy at times."

"I was hoping to see you, Miss Lady. I can come to you, or you can come to me. It makes no difference just as long as you tell me I can see you, and see you soon," he said.

"Well, how soon are you trying to see me, Mr. Giovanni," she flirted back, wanting to see him just as bad.

"Right now, girl," he laughed that sexy laugh she loved. "Why you think I'm calling? I been thinking about you a lot these days. I'm missing you and missing the taste of that sweet pussy." His voice became husky with lust, and the thought of her wetness caused him to pitch a tent in his jeans. "I wanna taste you again," he told her.

"Is that right," she said softly.

"Indeed, it is and maybe, maybe if I'm good, I can get past first base and find out what you feel like."

"Stop playing with me, Giovanni! You a mess babe," she said, smiling. "But, for real, I've been thinking about you too, Giovanni," she admitted.

"You know you sound so damn when you say my name."

"Oh yeah?" she replied, laughing like a school girl on the phone with her high school sweet heart. "Well, if you really wanna hear me say your name, give me a reason…"

"Now whose playing?" he said, enjoying where the conversation was headed. "How about we both stop playing games and see if we can make that happen? And even if it doesn't, I just really wanna see your beautiful face."

"Sounds good to me," Viviana said without hesitation. "I'll text you my address and you can be on your way then. What time should I expect you?"

"I can be there in within the hour," he said, confirming the date.

"Great, but before you go, is there anything special you'd like me to have for you to sip on?"

"Your juice is enough to quench my thirst, baby."

On the other end of the phone, Viviana could hardly contain herself. She couldn't believe how the two of them had clicked right from the start, and the best part of it all was she was genuinely feeling him.

"Nah, but seriously, I'll have whatever you're having; it's your night," Giovanni finally told her.

"Okay, that works for me. And, don't worry, I have excellent taste in all things," she laughed. "So, I guess I'll see you when you get here?"

"Most definitely. And don't *you* worry," he added flipping her words on her. "You have no idea how your life is about to change. From this night on, and for as long as you'll let me, I'm gonna make sure you have the best time of your life while you fuckin' with me." His tone was serious and sincere, and for some reason Viviana knew she could believe him.

"I like the sound of that. Hurry up and get here, I can't wait to see you," she told him.

"Okay, Miss Lady, I'll see you soon."

"Okay, see you then," she replied and ended the call.

By the time she'd hung up, her panties were completely wet, so she rushed to shower to freshen up, ready to see what the night would bring.

———

Later that evening, Giovanni entered the address Viviana had sent him, into his GPS system and headed over to her place. When he arrived, she had gone all out for him. The dining room table was beautifully set for two and there were scented candles sitting right in the middle. There were lobster tails with Italian pasta, tomato salad, and red wine.

They laughed and conversed playfully over dinner and flirted in between sips of wine. Afterwards, they moved the intimate party for two to the living room, where they sat and chilled on the sofa. Viviana had the music playing softly through the PA system.

"You have a beautiful home, Viviana," Giovanni told her as he moved in closer toward her.

"Thank you," she said, modestly.

"No, really… you have good taste, Ms. Lady, and the atmosphere is nice in here," he added, as he looked around.

Wanting him to see the exterior setup, she escorted him outside through the sliding glass door and over to the pool area, one of her favorite spots of the house. A huge indigo lit Infinity pool that looked off into the beautiful view of North Shore Ocean sat right outside the patio.

"This is so relaxing," Viviana," he said, as he grabbed her and held her close to him. "I could grow to love this, and even more, I could grow to love you," he said, looking deeply in her eyes. "You tryna make a nigga fall in love, girl." He kissed her gently and stopped.

"What's wrong, Giovanni?" she wondered.

"Nothin' baby. I was just thinking about how I can't wait to spoil you, and how I can't wait for you to be all mine."

"So, what makes you think I'm not already all yours?"

Before he could answer, she leaned in and continued the kiss right where it had left off then smiled coyly. Hand in hand they walked back inside, and back to the sofa.

They sat down, and he placed his arms around her—she snuggled up against him as if in his arms was where she belonged. The music played softly in the background and something about the atmosphere made her feel all warm and cozy inside.

"So, do you feel like I'm the type of man you could get serious with?" he asked in his deep, sexy voice, "can I *be* your man?"

Viviana felt as if there were a million butterflies fluttering around inside her, and her heart beat rapidly. Love was the last thing she'd been looking for, and she'd been hurt a time or two in the past. However, as strange as it may have seemed, with Giovanni, it had truly been love at first sight. She couldn't deny the way he made her feel, even though she hadn't known him that long. *Am I crazy?* she thought silently. *Has being without a man for so long caused me to be vulnerable?* All these thoughts and more lingered in her mind, but still, it felt so right.

She knew she had to say something, and she had always been the kind of woman who got what she wanted. She sat up on the sofa and moved her face in closer to his.

"Yes, Giovanni, baby! Yes, I would love for you to be my man," she said before she could second-guess herself. She brushed a finger across his chin and gave him the biggest kiss ever.

Giovanni took her hands in his and planted soft kisses all over them before making his way to her lips.

"Mmm, Giovanni… your lips are so soft," she said between kisses. She grabbed his face and began kissing him harder, and deeper. Viviana looked into Giovanni's eyes as if she had been hypnotized. "What have you done to me?" she asked, as if she could hardly get the words out.

"What have I done to you?" he repeated. "The question is what have you done to me, Viviana? I'm usually not like this with any woman, but it seems like you've put some kind of spell on me," he whispered seductively. "I love the way you handle things," he said, taking her by surprise.

Taken aback, he his words had caught her completely off guard. "What do you mean by that? You said that as if you know me personally or something?" she added, "like you been watching me or something..."

Giovanni simply smiled and planted another kiss on her lips, then her face, then her eyes, and then he grabbed her hand, and again he kissed it. Viviana was so overwhelmed with happiness, she hadn't even realize he had never answered her question. And that was exactly the way Giovanni wanted it.

Viviana had no idea the man she was falling so hard for was the exact same man who had been buying up all the keys she'd been flooding the streets with. While she was queen on one coast, he was king on the other. So, when Giovanni told her he was a business man, she really had no clue as to how much alike they truly were; nevertheless, she would soon she would find out. . .

Taking him by the hand, she led him up the stairs to her bedroom and over to her California king size bed.

Giovanni looked around and smiled as he pulled her closer toward him. "This is nice, baby... I see you really doin' ya' thing. You livin' nice, got your own deli and clothing store... It makes me happy to see a strong, black woman holdin' her own. It's so attractive," he said.

Viviana whispered in his ear, "Yes, I do live nice," then she pushed him back on the bed.

When he tried to sit up and take control, she wasn't having it. "Uh-uh, playboy, it's my turn now," she said, smiling deviously.

Wanting to oblige her every wish, he fell back on the bed and she proceeded to undress them both. Afterwards, she took her left hand and began to rub on his massive man-hood. Giovanni was blessed, and his dick was thick and long; the veins sticking out looked like little worms growing underneath the skin.

Giovanni let out a deep moan as he bit down on his bottom lip. Viviana was making him feel so good, the simple touch of her hand nearly made his knees go weak, and this was very unlike him.

Before he could stop himself, he reached around and smacked her on the ass hard, then he grabbed her breasts and began sucking on her nipples.

"Mmm... mmm... Giovanni, you know I like when you suck on my nipples... oh my God, baby," she cried out.

She climbed on top of him and planted kisses all over his chest before making her way down to his hardness. At first, she teased him just as he'd done her during their first encounter. She kissed it softly, gently, and used her tongue to lick up and down the length of his shaft. Then she took him in her mouth and began sucking slowly up, and then down, up and down... Making sure it was good and wet, she allowed the saliva from her mouth to drip on the head as she sucked faster and harder, while using her hands to squeeze on his nuts.

By now, Giovanni's toes had begun to curl, and deep moans escaped his lips. When Viviana took all of him, inch by inch inside her mouth and deep-throated him, he almost lost it. Her tongue danced around the head as her hand simultaneously jacked him off.

"You are mi-mine," he said breathlessly.

"You like that, baby?" she asked as she massaged his sack.

Giovanni rolled her over and mounted himself on top of her. He looked her in the eyes and kissed her more passionately than he ever had before. He pulled her hair to the side and nibbled on her earlobe. Wanting to taste every inch of her body, he sucked and bit lightly her neck. Using his hand, he to explore her breasts, he pinched each nipple before sucking one after the other.

Finally, his head made its way down to her wetness and he stuck his tongue right in the center and twirled it around. Viviana moaned and groaned as her body responded to his touch.

"Viviana, you taste so good," he whispered, as he made slurping sounds trying to lick up every drop of her juices. "You sure you ready for this?" he asked sincerely.

"Ohh, yes, baby... Please, Giovanni," she begged, "I need to feel you inside me now, baby," she cooed lustfully.

He rose up and guided himself inside her slowly, and her breath caught in her throat when she nearly screamed from the size. Slowly, he rocked her, pushing himself deeper inside her, inch by inch. He knew he was larger than average and he wanted this moment to be special for the both of them. First, he grinded in slow motion, but with each stroke, he increased the pace.

Viviana's pussy became so wet it started to make slurping noises. Giovanni reached underneath her and held her ass cheeks apart and started stroking her harder and faster.

"Oh yes, yes, Giovanni... fuck me, baby," she pleaded. "Make love to me, Giovanni-van-nni," she panted breathlessly.

"Work that pussy, girl," he demanded in a raspy tone, "this pussy gonna make a nigga go crazy," he told her, as he pounded relentlessly. "Tell me this my pussy, Viviana," he said, "tell me!"

"Yes, yes... its yours baby, nobody else's!" she shouted out.

"I will kill you if you ever fuck around on me, you hear me!" he asked. "This pussy is mine, and I'm yours, you hear me Viviana?"

"Yes, Giovanni, baby, I hear you! I'm yours baby, this pussy belongs to you!"

Hearing her say those words caused something to snap in Giovanni. He grabbed her by the legs and put each one over his shoulders, and stroked her real slow, before he commenced to beating it up, hitting it harder, faster, and deeper. By now the headboard had started hitting against the wall.

"I'ma 'bout to cum, Giovanni! Fuck me…fuck me… I'm cummin', baby!"

"I'ma 'bout to cum too, baby, and I'ma bust this nut all in you," he said, right before he released. "Ughhh… oh shit, girl!" he yelled out.

"Giovanni, oh God, yes!"

"That shit was good," Giovanni told her once they'd both climaxed. He rolled over and kissed her lips and wrapped his arms around her.

She lay in his arms breathing heavily, and soon they both dozed off fast to sleep.

CHAPTER 7

Viviana arrived at her clothing store 11 o'clock on Monday Morning. When she entered, the girls noticed something different about her. She was all smiles and she had an unusual glow about her. It was very unlike her, especially on a Monday, everybody hated Mondays. Not only was it the start of the work week, but because Viviana was the boss, her duties entailed a lot more. She scrolled in with a stride that made her appear as if she were walking on clouds.

"Good morning ladies!" she said cheerfully.

Everyone greeted her and said hello. Of course, Sharon and Sandra wanted details so as soon as Viviana headed to her office, the two were right on heels.

Viviana looked them both up and down and asked, "Damn, what's goin' on? Why y'all runnin' up in my office like that?"

Waiting to hear their response, she takes her seat behind her desk and takes a sip of her Columbian coffee.

Sandra and her sister eye one another then they eye Viviana curiously.

"What?" she said, looking at the two of them strangely. "What's wrong with you guys? Is everything Okay?"

Sharon threw her hand up in the air and laughed. "Yes, girl, everything is fine with us. We were just wondering what's up with you, Miss Thang?"

"We see that glow on your face, plus you came up in here lookin' like you just won the lottery or some shit," Sandra added. "You musta had a really great time while you were away!"

Viviana's smile grew even bigger, but before telling her cousins the real reason for her smile, she thought it'd be fun to make them wait awhile.

She put her car keys away in her desk drawer and took her files from the folder she'd left on her desk the last time she was there.

"I don't know what you two talkin' about. I'm not actin' any different than usual if you ask me. I mean, I saw my mother and I went to visit my aunt in Colombia, so I guess I'm just happy that's all," she said followed by a light chuckle.

Sharon looked at Sandra and twisted her lips to said as if to say, *"Yeah right."* Come on, Viv we know you, you can't fool us," she said.

"Y'all so damn nosy! Why y'all all up in my business?" she asked playfully before she burst out laughing hysterically. "Okay, heffas, if y'all must know… I met this guy and I think I'm in love with him! There, I said it!" she blurted out.

Sharon and Sandra both started screaming and clapping as if *they* had won the lottery. The way they were acting, you'd think Viviana had told them she was getting married.

"Damn, you bitches act like I ain't never had no man before," she said as they all continued laughing.

"No, we know better than that, Cuzzie. It's just that we know you been through a lot and we just happy for you, boo," Sharon explained. She got up and walked over to give Viviana a hug.

"And you tell that nigga he better not hurt you or we gonna fuck his ass up," Sandra said.

Viviana was so happy, she couldn't help but to cry. For once in her life she felt like things were finally coming together for her; business was good, and now she had a man to enjoy life with.

The three of them joined in on group hug as she and her cousins shared in her happiness.

"Why the hell you cryin'?" Sandra asked.

"Girl, these are tears of joy," she answered as she wiped the tears away. "Y'all know I couldn't wait to get back and tell you, but we'll talk later. "Get on outta here and go help the other ladies out in the store. I love you guys so much," she told them.

She walked them to the door and kissed them each on the cheek before they walked out of her office.

1:00 p.m. Bank Run and Lunch

Viviana was just finishing up a phone conversation when Sharon entered back into her office. She didn't want to interrupt, so she took a seat at the desk and waited quietly until Viviana was done with her call.

"What's up, girl?" she asked once she'd hung up the phone. "How is everything going out on the floor?"

"Busy as hell as always, normal day at Belladonnas," Sharon replied, "but I came in here to tell you that this guy came in and bought up almost ten thousand dollars of merchandise."

"Oh really?" Viviana asked.

"Yeah, Viv, a very sexy, tall, handsome, flyy dude too!"

"I guess I missed that one," Viviana said, as she scrolled though the computer's spread sheets but still didn't see the sale Sharon was referring to. "That's a blessing that he spent so much money with us," she told Sharon.

"Yeah, I'm happy about that, Viv, and he was actually the first customer to spend that much in one day!"

"Well, that's a good thing, and either way, we're thankful for all of our customers, because that's how y'all get paid," Viviana said, before turning her focus back on the computer.

Glancing over the sales of the day, she said, "Not bad at all, especially for a Monday."

"I told you, Viv, we been busy out there today, boss!" Sharon reiterated.

"Well, I think it's time for me to make a quick bank run, and pick up something for lunch, so go ask the girls what they want and write everyone's order down. I'll be out there in a few to get it," Viviana said.

Not long after, she locked up her office and stopped by the counter where Sharon and Sandra were. Sharon handed her a list for Subway and continued ringing up customers.

Viviana let the girls know she'd be back within an hour and headed for the door.

"Hello, how are you today? Thank you for shopping at Belladonna's, have a great afternoon," she said, as she walked by customers shopping in her store.

2:30 p.m.

When Viviana got back with lunch, she handed Sandra the bag from Subway and told the ladies she would take over until after lunch. Sandra looked in the bag and saw four turkey subs and turned to go to the breakroom.

"You're welcome, Sandra," Viviana said jokingly.

"Oh, my bad," Sandra laughed. "Thank you, ma'am," she turned around and called out to Viviana.

All the ladies sat in the breakroom and laughed and talked about the busy day they had. "My feet are killing me," one of them said.

"Mine are too," another agreed."

Just as they were finishing up, the bell sounded letting them know break was over.

"Okay, everyone back to work," Viviana said when she noticed them coming out from break.

Back in her office, Viviana placed a few more calls and continued handling the corporate part of the store's business. She glanced at the clock on the wall and realized she hadn't heard from Felix in a while. *Something isn't right,* she thought, *and Felix is keeping something from me. I will get to the bottom of this real soon, as a matter of fact, let me call this nigga.*

She grabbed her cell phone from her purse and dialed Felix's number but received no answer. She called it again, and still, no answer.

"This muthafucka better be hurt or something," she mumbled. She put her cell phone away and sat back in her office chair. She was beyond pissed. She couldn't quiet put her finger on it, but whatever Felix was up to had better not cause any problems for her father's empire, because if it did, he was going to have to deal with her and her entire family. Looking around in her office, she thought to herself as her mind drifted off in a daze. *This nigga don't want no problems. I already told his ass, cousin or no cousin, his ass will get kicked out the game messin' with me.*

The store stayed busy for the remainder of the day and everyone was glad when it was finally closing time. After following the usual closing procedures, everyone said their good nights and went their separate ways. Not long after, Viviana locked up for the night and headed home.

───────

Viviana arrived home and used the remote to open the garage before pulling in. After parking her car, she hopped out and walked to the door to let herself inside the house. Upon entering, she sat down at the island in the kitchen to look over the mail.

"Bills on top of bills," she said out loud, as she threw all the envelopes down on the counter.

She headed up to her room and flopped down on her bed, allowing her body to fall in a backwards position. She was so exhausted, she could hardly wait to take a hot shower. She took her clothes off and headed to the bathroom, grabbing her robe on the way.

After she showered, she went back down the stairs to watch a little television before bed. She had been hearing about the movie Killumba and figured tonight would be as good a night as any to watch it. Grabbing her Roku remote, she got comfortable on the sofa, set the TV on the YouTube Channel, and browsed until she found the movie.

Just as she was about to get relaxed, her cell phone rang. She sat up and ran to the kitchen where she'd left her phone lying on the kitchen island; she knew it couldn't be Giovanni because she had set a special ring tone to go with his number. Looking at the caller, she realized it was her cousin Felix. *Now his dumbass decides to call.*

"Hello," she answered with an attitude.

"What's up, girl?" he asked in a nonchalant tone.

"What you want Felix? I been trying to reach you all day," she told him.

"I know, Viv… I had this lil' bitch over and we been gettin' it in all day," he said and laughed.

"OK. And?" Viviana replied. "Felix, I haven't heard from you since the last time we talked and we really need to sit down and have a heart to heart on some real serious shit, man, for real."

"Oh, Lord, here we go," he said, as if Viviana was the one with the problem. "What I do now?" Felix rolled his eyes on the other end as he waited on an answer.

"It's what you're *not* doin' in this business that we need to discuss, Felix! We have to stay connected and you haven't been doing that lately," she explained further.

"What you mean, Viv?" he asked defensively. "Sound like you tryna say I ain't handlin' business." Felix's facial expression had turned to a frown and he didn't like the tone Viviana had been using with him during their last few conversations.

However, Viviana had had just about enough of her cousin's bullshit and it was really starting to annoy her.

"I mean exactly what I said, Felix! You're not communicating with me like you used to and I'm starting to feel some type of way about it! So, we need to sit down face to face," she repeated.

"Okay, okay, Cuz," he said hiding his true feelings. We can meet up somewhere tomorrow. I'll call you with the time and place," he assured her.

"Alright, Cuzzo," Viviana said reluctantly, "and yo ass better answer yo' phone, nigga!"

Felix laughed off Viviana's seriousness like always and told her he'd see her tomorrow before hanging up.

CHAPTER 8

The weekend had finally arrived, and Viviana walked the dock of North Shore as she waited on Felix to arrive. It was such a beautiful evening out and she was enjoying the atmosphere. The birds were flying high on the beach, the waves were rolling in on the ocean, and it was so peaceful.

She looked at her watch to check the time and realized Felix was late yet again. Since she was actually enjoying the calmness and peace of the ocean, it didn't really bother her that he hadn't showed up yet.

Leaning her body up against the railing, she closed her eyes and let the sound of the ocean take her mind away from all the stress in her life. She enjoyed her life and she counted everyday as a blessing from God; nonetheless, it was tiresome and stressful owning two thriving businesses and living the life of a drug queen and overseer of an empire. She cherished moments like these because they were far and few in-between. She opened her eyes and noticed Felix walking toward her on the dock.

"What's up, Felix," she greeted when he was closer.

"Hey, Viv. What's up," he replied. Reaching out to give her a huge.

"Let's take a walk," she suggested.

They walked off the dock and onto the beach, away from the crowd of beachgoers, where they could talk privately.

Once they felt they had walked far enough away, Viviana wasted no time getting right to point. "Felix, I'm not gonna beat around the bush 'cause like I said, this is serious to me… now you my family and all," she started, "my blood, and I love you dearly, you my right-hand man, but when you told me you let the guy who bought the ounces from you see the key you cut it from, that disturbed me really badly," she told him openly and honestly.

"I know it did, Cuz, and I told you it would never happen again," Felix said in his defense. "True, I fucked up!" he admit. "I did, and it's my fault, please forgive me for that."

Felix's voice was sincere and his usual habit of laughing things off didn't exist at the moment. He knew he had fucked up, and he knew he would have to prove to Viviana that it was an honest, senseless mistake on his part. But, before he could begin to do that, he needed her to understand the situation for what it was, so he continued explaining.

"Listen, Cuz, I need to continue gettin' this money for you and *me*," he emphasized. "Don't count me out, Viv… I don't know what I was thinkin' Cuz." He looked down as a show of his shame.

Viviana knew he was sorry, so she reached over and lifted his head with her finger. "I forgive you Felix, and I truly accept your apology, but—she paused before continuing, "one thing I'm tellin' you now and I'm speaking from the heart, shit like that *cannot* happen again. Suppose that same nigga came back one day and robbed you or killed you?" she asked seriously.

"You right Viv," he said, shaking his head at the mere thought. He rubbed his hands against his face and looked his cousin in the eyes.

"And on top of that, my father's empire could be in jeopardy, did you think about that?" she asked.

"True, Viv, and there's nothin' else I can say except you right, Viv."

"This is my last and only time sayin' this to you. I love you, but it can't happen again or you out!" she said with finality.

"It won't happen again, Viv," he said. He reached out his arms and she excepted his embrace.

"I'ma get out of here now," she said.

Felix put his Ray Bans shades back over his eyes and kissed Viviana on the cheek. She puts her Prada shades back on returned a kiss to his cheek.

They walked back up to the dock to leave and said their goodbyes. "Holla at me, Cuz," Felix said as he walked off to his car.

Viviana got inside her Audi, ready to pull off and her cell phone rang.

"Hello," she answered in an excited tone.

"Hello, beautiful lady," Giovanni's voice boomed through the receiver.

"Hi, baby!" she yelled out.

"How you been?" he asked.

"I'm good, baby, just thinking about you," she told him.

"Same here," Giovanni replied, "you always on my mind, girl."

"Oh really," she flirted.

"Yes, really," he laughed. "So, where are you?"

"I had met my cousin Felix out here to North Shore Beach to talk and I had just got in my car to leave when you called," she explained.

"Oh, okay. But look, I need you to meet me at the airport in two hours," he informed her. "I wanna take you somewhere special."

"Are you serious," she asked in a surprised tone.

"Yes, I'm serious, babe. I told you I wanna treat you like the Queen you are. Let me take care of you," he told her in his deep voice. "Okay, baby," Viviana replied softly through the phone. "But, what should I wear? What should I bring?" she asked excitedly.

"Viviana, you so sexy, you look beautiful in anything you wear, so just bring yourself and something for the night. I'll take care of the rest," he answered with authority.

"Okay, Giovanni, baby, but where are we going?" she asked curiously.

"You'll just have to be at the airport to find out, now won't you?" Giovanni laughed.

Viviana smiled and agreed to meet him in two hours and they ended the call. With a big smile on her face, she put her car in reverse and headed home to grab an overnight bag.

———————

Twenty- minutes later, she pulled into the garage to park the car. She was so excited, she had smiled all the way home. Jumping out of the car, she nearly skipped to the door like a school girl in love. She entered the house and threw her bag and keys on the table before running up the stairs to her bedroom.

When she walked into the room, she couldn't believe her eyes. There were red roses and rose petals lying throughout the room. On her bed was a note, and there was a bottle of her favorite wine chilling on ice sitting on her nightstand. The note read: *To the most beautiful, sexy, sweetest person I have ever met. May your life be filled with so much joy and happiness, I would love to make all your dreams come true if you would let me. I have wine chilling for you as you prepare to take this elevation of life with me. Get ready! Love Giovanni…*

She sat on her bed and allowed her tears to flow freely. She felt so much joy inside, she couldn't have stopped them if she wanted to. *This man is so amazing,* she thought fondly. Again, she was so caught up in how he was making her feel, it never dawned on her that he had somehow found a way to let himself inside her house.

She went in her closet, grabbed a change of clothes, and rushed to the bathroom to take a quick shower.

An hour later, she was ready and looking fabulous. Dressed in a black Fendi cat suit and Fendi heels, she decided to rock her Fendi clutch and Fendi accessories. *Damn I look good,* she thought, admiring herself in front of the full-length mirror.

She rushed down the stairs with her Fendi overnight bag in hand, and she was about to set the alarm when her phone rang.

"Hello?" she answered. "Hi, Giovanni is anything wrong, babe?"

"No, just a little change of plans," he said.

Viviana sighed deeply and sat down on her sofa, trying to remain calm. She crossed her fingers and hoped Giovanni wasn't calling to with bad news that would cause them to have to cancel their plans.

"Well, nothin' is wrong, it's just that I have a limo outside waitin' on you, to bring you to the airport so you won't have to drive, baby," he said in a cool, collective tone.

"Don't scare me like that, babe! I thought you were calling to tell me our plans had been canceled." On the verge of tears, she allowed the huge smile to take its place back on her face.

"Oh no, baby, you're coming with me for sure! I just wanted you to be able to enjoy the ride babe, that's all," he told her. "I'm sorry if I scared you."

"Aww, Giovanni, you sent a limo for me, thank you," she said, letting out a sigh of relief.

"Yes, I did, and you're welcome. Now go on out front because he's outside waiting on you," he told her.

"OK, I'm going now. Thanks again, baby. You're the best," she said before hanging up.

CHAPTER 9

The limo driver pulled up to the Teterboro Private Airport, and Giovanni stood by the private jet looking handsome in his Black Gucci suit dripping in diamonds.

When the driver opened the door for Viviana, she stepped out and made her way over to Giovanni. She greeted him with a warm embrace as he looked her up and down, marveling at how sexy she was dressed.

He pulled her into him and kissed her as if he hadn't seen her in years. He took her by the hand and guided her over to the steps of the jet.

"You lead the way," he said, allowing her to take the lead.

Once they were inside the plane, Viviana looked around in awe. "Wow, baby this jet is flyy!" she said like a little child on Christmas day.

She took a seat as she continued admiring the interior of the plane. The entire interior was all white, and she noticed the bottle of Rosè Moscato chilling on ice. What she didn't know was, Giovanni was a made-man, his money was long and there was nothing under the sun he couldn't have if he so desired.

He leaned in and planted a kiss on her forehead. "So, you like this jet, huh, baby?" he asked.

"Yes, I do," she said, "you have taste almost as good as mine," she laughed jokingly.

"Well, I'm glad you approve," he chuckled. "I picked this one out just for us," he told her with a smile.

Viviana looked at him curiously as she placed her Fendi overnight bag on the floor. "What do you mean you picked it out for us?"

"I mean it's ours!" he said as if were nothing, "this jet belongs to you and me… I bought it for us, babe," he said, giving her another kiss.

He took the bottle of Rosé Moscato out of the ice bucket and poured some into the two champagne flutes he had gotten just for the two of them.

"Giovanni, I can't believe this. I'm so happy right now, baby," she said as she grabbed his face and planted little kisses all over him.

"Whenever you want this jet, baby, take it… whether you need it for business, just chillin' with your girls, it'll always be available and fueled up for you. It's yours to use for whatever you want," Giovanni told her.

"Giovanni, baby, you're spoiling me." She blushed.

"Well, then, I guess my plan is working 'cause spoiling you is exactly what I wanna do." He smiled.

"You gonna mess around and make me fall in love with you," she said seriously.

"I hope so, Viviana," he said as he looked her in her eyes.

He reached over and grabbed her hand and held it tightly. The pilot announced for them to fasten their seat belts and let them know it was time for takeoff. As he did so, Giovanni refilled the flutes with champagne, and lifted it high in the air to make a toast.

"Here's to our future, together baby. Let's make it the best days of our lives," he said, tapping his flute against hers.

"Cheers to us," Viviana said, as she sipped the bubbly.

"You still ain't told me where we goin', baby?" she said to Giovanni with dreamy eyes.

Giovanni turned his focus toward the window and pretended not to hear her. When he looked back at her, her eyes twinkled like a child in a candy store as she waited on his response.

"Baby, please tell me," she cooed.

"Okay, I'm dying to tell you anyways," he said. "We're going to Paris, my love." He winked at her while giving her a hand a tender squeeze.

"Oh my, Giovanni! Really, baby? I've always dreamed of going there," she said as her eyes filled with happy tears.

Giovanni turned to look at her closely and the look in his eyes turned to a serious expression, and he was no longer playful.

"I just want to love you forever, Viviana… I want to spend the rest of my life with you," he said.

His sudden declaration of wanting to spend the rest of his life with her, took Viviana by total surprise. Although she had felt something for him from the start, she had no idea, he truly felt the same for her. Feeling a mixture of fear and happiness, Viviana's heart began to beat rapidly, and her breathing quickened.

"So, what are you saying, Giovanni?" she asked inquisitively.

Giovanni stuck his hand in his pocket, and he pulled out a little black box.

"Oh my God, Giovanni!" What is that, baby?" Viviana asked, holding her hand against her chest.

Taking his seatbelt off, he proceeded to bend on one knee. Looking Viviana deeply in her eyes, he grabbed her hand into his and held it close to his heart before speaking.

"Baby," he began, "ever since the moment I first laid eyes on you, I knew I had to someday make you mine. Something about the way you looked sitting on that bar stool with that big pretty smile, made me want to know more about you. A man like me never believed in love at first sight until I saw you," he said. "I think I loved you at 'hello'." Giovanni's voice seemed to crack from the passion he poured into each word and it was evident he was speaking from his heart and his words were sincere.

"But, Giovanni, baby, we've only known each other for six months. How can you love me that much, babe?" she asked in disbelief.

Giovanni looked at Viviana and held her face in his hands as if it were a delicate flower. "Viviana, you really don't know who I am do you?" he asked as he stared at her intently.

"No, Giovanni. Who are you. . .   really?" Viviana was confused and it showed on her expression.

"Giovanni kissed her gently on her lips. "Baby, I have a confession to make, and I hope you won't be too upset with me," he explained. "I've been knowing you for a long time now and it was only a matter of time that the day would come when we would finally meet."

"But, how, babe?" she asked.

"Wait, Viv, just hear me out, baby." Giovanni grew silent and the look on his face was one of sadness. He sighed heavily and shook his head slowly.

"What is it, baby? Tell me," Viviana demanded. "You're scaring me, Giovanni . . ."

"No, baby. . . don't be scared. I'm here to protect you, and I'm going to live the rest of my life making sure I do. That's what I promised your father before he died."

Viviana's mouth dropped open wide and her words seem to get caught in her throat. She covered her mouth with her hand because she couldn't believe what she was hearing. Who was this man? How did he know her father? She gathered her thoughts and found her voice again.

"My father? What do you mean, Giovanni? How do you know my father?" she asked, as her eyes welled with tears.

"Well, your father was a very well-known and powerful man. I was his hitman, Viviana."

"Oh my God! Viviana said, allowing the tears to flow freely.

Giovanni reached out and took her hand in his as he continue to tell her about his past. "I was his hitman and I did a lot of business for your father. I don't think he ever thought someone would actually murder him, one day as we were sitting in his office, he told me if anything ever happened to him to make sure I look after his Empire, and to take care of his daughter. . . . You."

Viviana began to cry harder as she realized that even in his death, her father was still watching over her. "Oh my God, Giovanni, I didn't know any of this."

"See, babe, your father was a very private man. I see a lot of him in you and that's one of the thing I love that about you. So, you see, I've always loved you, Viviana. The first time I saw you, you had come by his office as I was leaving. You didn't see me, but I fell in love with you as soon as I laid eyes on you," he said sincerely. "Before your father died, I asked for permission to have your hand in marriage if the time ever presented itself, and he said yes, and he gave me his blessing. So, you see, baby, you and I are meant to be together. We were destined to be long ago before either of us even knew it. I love you, Viviana. You've become my world, and I need you in my life for as long as I live. 'Til death do us part, baby."

Giovanni wiped her tears away and kissed her passionately, softly, gently.

"You waited for me all this time, Giovanni?" she asked through her tears.

"Yes, baby, and now that I've gotten you, I'm not ever letting you go, not ever."

"Aww, Giovanna. I love you forever, baby," she told him.

They embraced one another tightly, and from that moment on, they knew theirs was a bond that could never be broken.

Eight hours later, Viviana's and Giovanni's jet had landed, and they were driven to the Shangri-La Hotel in Paris, France.

"May I take your bags, sir?" the door attendant asked.

"No, I think we can handle it," Giovanni said, "but thank you anyway."

The two walked hand and hand to the elevator and waited for it to come down. Once they boarded, they rode it to the 28th floor.

"Babe, this hotel is beautiful," Viviana said as she looked around at all the beautiful marble fixtures and paintings inside the elevator.

"I know, right," Giovanni agreed. "I'm pleased you like it since it was the only hotel I could get on such short notice.

"Well, Giovanni, babe, I absolutely love it," Viviana said with a smile.

The bell of the elevator rang, and the elevator doors opened, letting them know they had reached their floor. Giovanni pulled the luggage behind him as they walked down the hallway in search of room 2804. They made it halfway down the long hallway when they noticed their room number on the wall to the right of them.

"Here it is," Giovanni said stopping in front of the door. He handed the key to Viviana and allowed her to enter first.

She opened the door and was instantly amazed at the beauty inside. "This is spectacular, baby, I love it!" she told him. "It must've cost a fortune," she guessed.

"The price doesn't matter," he said coolly. "All that matters is that you love it and you enjoy our stay here. My only goal is to make you feel special on this special day."

Out of nowhere, he reached out and grabbed her by the waist and kissed her softly before getting down on one knee. Viviana was totally taken aback and wanted to pinch herself to be sure she wasn't dreaming.

"So… what's your answer?" he asked, "Will you be my wife and love me for the rest of our lives?" he asked again.

"Yes, Giovanni, yes, I will be your wife," she answered as her tears flowed freely. She crouched down so they were face to face and kissed him with all the passion she could muster.

He then picked her up and took her to the beautiful royal bed and began removing her clothes slowly. Placing soft, delicate kisses all over her, he whispered how much he loved her.

"I love you, baby," she told him as she looked him in his eyes. Please, don't ever stop loving me, please don't baby."

Giovanni caressed her body tightly and removed his clothes and the two of them climbed in bed. The flight had been long and both of them were tired, so now, they lay next to one another exhausted and in love.

Viviana snuggled closely against his chest as she closed her eyes to dream of life being his wife. Gently, he rubbed his fingertip on her temples and soon she was fast asleep. He kissed her on the forehead and not long after, he had fallen asleep too.

———————

Viviana and Giovanni lay soundly sleeping. They had fallen asleep almost as soon as they had entered their room, and they slept through the entire night. A knock at the door stirred them from their sleep as the voice on the other side called out, "Room service!"

Giovanni opened his eyes and sat up. He stretched and yawned as he looked at a sleeping Viviana and smiled. Realizing he needed to answer the door, he quickly jumped up and grabbed his Versace robe After putting it on, he went to the door.

"Who is it?" he asked, as he tied the robe.

"Room service, sir," the bellhop answered.

He opened the door and remembered the order he had placed the night before. "Good morning," he said extending his hand. "Come on in," he told the bellhop.

The gentleman pushed the food cart into their room and asked if that would be all. After lifting the lids, he Giovanni approved the order and gave the man a hefty tip for his service.

"Thank you, sir," the man said before leaving the room.

Giovanni locked the door and walked to the bed to wake Viviana.

She opened her eyes and greeted her man with a huge smile. Climbing out of bed, she headed to the bathroom to brush her teeth and wash her face.

Once she was done, she followed Giovanni out to the balcony and leaned in for a kiss.

"Good morning, baby," he said. "I thought we could eat out here this morning and take in the view of beautiful Paris."

"Yes, baby, we can do that. This is nice," she replied as she took her a seat at the lovely draped in white.

"This view is amazing, babe," Viviana said.

Giovanni had thought of everything, and he thought a nice glass of mimosa was just what they needed to start the morning off right. He filled two glasses and handed one over to Viviana.

"Thank you, baby," she said, leaning over to kiss him.

"Ummm, baby, you're welcome," he said.

"Look at this view, babe," Viviana said as she looked down from the balcony and into the city.

"Yes, it's beautiful out here, isn't it?" he replied as he began to load his plate with food.

"Everything looks so good," Viviana said. "We have fruits, veggies, eggs, bagels, steak, coffee, tea... there's so much food, I don't know where to start," she laughed.

When she noticed Giovanni fixing his plate, she smacked his hand playfully. "You've done enough, let me do that for you. Just tell me what you want, babe. I got you," she told him.

"I want some of those eggs and a piece of that ribeye steak," she said looking at the variety of dishes. "I'll also have some of that fruit too, babe," he said.

She fixed his plate and handed it to him nicely before fixing a plate for herself.

"There's so much food, Giovanni! Why did you order all this?" she asked.

"Well, because I didn't know what you really liked so I ordered everything on the breakfast menu," he said honestly.

"Giovanni, that was so sweet of you," she said taking a bite of the steak. I don't know what I'ma do with you, baby." She looked at him and smiled sincerely.

"Just love me… that's all I want you to do for me," he said and gave her a cool wink.

"Giovanni let me ask you a question," she said.

"Yes, babe, what is it?" he asked curiously.

"How the hell you get in my house to put those roses and wine in there?" As she waited on his reply, she put a piece of the melon in her mouth.

"Well, dear," he explained, "you know I got a lot of power in them streets. And because of that power, I got a few connects in the security business," he told her.

"Ohhh, I see," she said with a smirk. "I guess that answer is good enough for me."

"I love you, Viviana Moreno," he blurted out.

"I love you too, Giovanni."

"Look, Viv, when we get married, I know you'll probably want to keep your father's last name and—.

"No, Giovanni," she quickly cut him off, "I want your last name. Nothing would make me happier!"

"Seriously?" he asked as if he were surprised.

"Yes, seriously. I know that's what my father would've wanted."

"You're right. And besides, I like the sound of Viviana Lucus," he said. They both burst out laughing because they knew that's what Giovanni wanted all along.

"Okay, enough of this already. Let's go inside and get dressed so we can go see the town," he said.

"And, do a little shopping," she added.

Giovanni led the way back inside and Viviana followed behind him. He wanted the day to be special yet fun, and although Viviana could afford anything she wanted, she had forgotten what it felt like to have a man spoil her. However, Giovanni was just the man for the job; he wanted to lavish her with all the finer things in life and give her whatsoever her heart desired.

For starters, he began their outing by taking her on shopping spree all around the town. Paris was well-known for its boutiques and designer stores, and a lot of the designers themselves were natives of Paris. Sure, Viviana owned the finest fashions, bags and, shoes, but because these items were coming from Giovanni, she would treasure them even more.

Their first stop was to Rayore's, a very expensive clothing store for women. Some of the richest women of Paris could be seen frequenting the store and vacationers would walk by just to window shop. Viviana felt like the luckiest woman alive.

They walked in hand in hand and the salesman called out, "Welcome to Rayore's. Please, let me know if I can be of assistance!"

"Thank you," they responded, almost in unison.

"Babe, these clothes are hot," Viviana said excitedly.

She quickly released Giovanni's hand and took off walking ahead of him through the store. There was so much to choose from, she didn't know where to start looking first.

Picking out whatever she wanted as instructed, she carried her first selection of clothes to a nearby dressing room to try them on. Giovanni smiled as he tagged along behind her and sat on the bench outside the sitting area of the dressing room.

"I'll wait right here, and you can let me see how you look in everything," he said, "get anything you want in the store," he reminded her.

Viviana hurried into the dressing room all smiles as she began to try on everything from hats to shoes, and bags by every designer one could think of.

"I love everything on you, Viv," Giovanni said, complimenting her.

"Thank you, babe," she said, as she checked herself out in the mirror.

"You have everything you need, ma'am?" the sales clerk asked.

"Yes, sir. Thank you," Viviana told him politely.

"She's a lucky lady to have a man like you to buy her anything she wants," the sales clerk said, looking at Giovanni.

"No, sir… I'm the lucky one," Giovanni smiled.

"Are you ready to check out?" Giovanni asked Viviana.

"Yes, baby, I am," she replied with her arms full.

They took the items to the counter and the cashier rang them up.

"Will this be all, ma'am?" the sales clerk asked.

"Yes, this is it," she answered.

She smiled and leaned in to kiss Giovanni on the cheek. Once the items had been rang up. The sales clerk looked to Giovanni as if there was no way he could afford the purchase.

"Is something wrong?" he asked, noticing the look on the sales clerk face.

The sales clerk cleared his throat a few times and finally said, "Well, sir, Um-um… the total for your purchase is $25,185."

Giovanni didn't bat an eye, nor did he respond. He simply dug in his pocket, pulled out his wallet, and handed the man his Black American Express Unlimited Purchase Card in true baller style.

After going shopping at all the other stores, both, Giovanni, and Viviana were exhausted. So, they headed back to their room to get a little rest before ending the evening with a nice quiet dinner at Cinq Mars, where the atmosphere was laid back and welcoming. In fact, it reminded them of dining back at home, and both loved it. After having a lovely dinner, the two showered once more and made some good loving before drifting off to sleep in one another's arms.

CHAPTER 10

Giovanni kissed Viviana on her forehead while they lay together in his grey platform-based king size bed. The bed was huge with its 5 inches high grey leather pin cushion headboard that match the beautiful grey walls. The entire room was perfectly suited for a gentleman such as himself.

"I'm so happy to be home!" Giovanni exclaimed.

"Yes, baby, I am too," Viviana replied as she held him tightly.

Looking out of huge window, they had a picture-perfect view of Jersey Shore. The beautiful night lights of the city lit his room up making it a beautiful moment.

The next morning 10:00 a.m.

Viviana arrived at her store ready to get back to business.

"Good morning, ladies," she greeted the staff.

She wore the biggest smile on her face as she strolled through the doors, smiling from ear to ear.

"Good morning," the ladies called out. "Welcome back boss," Sharon said.

The ladies had been waiting for Viviana to return and they could hardly wait to find out what she'd been up to. As she headed toward her office, she could feel all eyes were on her. She stopped in her tracks and turned around eying the women one by one.

"What are y'all staring at?" she asked, trying hard not to laugh out.

"You got that same glow you had before, Viv," Sandra said, looking her up and down.

"Really, Sandra? Why what on earth are you talkin' about," she joked. "I don't know what *glow* you're referring to." All three of them rushed in her office and Sandra slammed the door behind them.

"What the hell Sandra?" Viv laughed out loud. "Why you slam my door like that, girl?"

Sandra and Sharon crossed their arms over their chest and tapped their feet to show their impatience. Of course, Viviana loved keeping her nosey cousins in suspense. She took her time and made herself a cup of coffee and then she sat down slowly behind her desk.

The girls didn't say a word, but their curiosity was about to drive them insane and they wanted to scream. Again, Viviana eyed them with a cute smile as she took her time booting on her laptops. When she took a sip of her coffee, both Sandra and Sharon could wait another minute.

"Viv, spill it, bitch!" Sharon said.

"Yeah, heffa," Sandra added. "You know what the hell we waitin' on! Tell us about the damn trip already!"

Viviana couldn't hold her laughter in any longer and she let out a laugh so loud, she was sure the customers had overheard her. Sharon and Sandra had to join in on the laughter as well.

"So, tell us what's up," Sandra asked, giving Viv her undivided attention. Sharon was all ears too.

"Y'all bitches are a mess, and nosey as hell," she said, once she finally stopped laughing. "Well, since y'all *must* know, his name is Giovanni," she told them.

"You mean the same guy who came in the store and purchased over $10,000 worth of stuff from us that day?" Sandra and Sharon look at one another baffled. "Wait a minute now, let me get this right… you talkin' about that fine ass nigga who bought up damn near everything?" she asked again for clarification.

"Yes girl! That's him," Viviana replied. "Why y'all act so surprised?" she asked, looking from Sandra to Sharon.

However, they were still in shock.

"Anyway, one night, me and Felix were chilling at the Sand Bar and he came up to me… he introduced himself and it's been a wrap since then," she said in a matter of fact kind of way. "Next thing I know, he invited me out on the town on a shopping spree to Paris. And check this out, y'all… we went on a private jet! Oh my God I had a wonderful time!"

"Really, Viv?" Oh my God Sandra said. It was easy to see she was genuinely excited for her cousin.

"Aww, Viv, I'm so happy for you," Sharon added.

"He stole my heart, y'all, and I think I'm in love. We've been spending a lot of time together and it's just been all love with him. He's so amazingly sweet to me and he treats me like a lady," she informed the girls.

"So, where he from with a name like that?" Sharon asked

"Oh, he from here, New Jersey."

"Well, tell us more," Sandra said inquisitively rubbing her hands together."

"Oh, no, that's all y'all gettin' from me today. Now get back to work," Viviana ordered. She attempted to look serious, but laughter got the best of her.

"Okay, okay," Sandra said, as she is got up from Viviana's desk.

"Alright, boss lady," Sharon said. "You can fill us in on the rest later."

Sharon and Sandra were so wrapped up in Viviana's love story, neither wanted to leave her office. Viviana promised they'd all catch up soon as she sent them on their way.

"I'll be out on the floor in a minute," she called out behind them as Sandra closed the door.

Viviana smiled and shook her head. She turned on her computer and began checking the sale and inventory for the days she'd been gone.

"Oh, my goodness," she mumbled, "business was good while I was gone."

She was proud of all of her staff, and especially, Sandra and Sharon. They always held things down when she needed them to and they never complained. As she sat at her desk deep in thought, Viviana had a great idea. *To show my appreciation, I think I'll surprise the girls and take them somewhere nice,* she thought to herself.

She looked down at the big calendar she kept taped to her desk to see when a good time would be to take the ladies on a trip. Standing up from her up from her desk, she rushed out of the office and headed to the counter where the ladies were ringing up customers.

"Hello, welcome to Belladonna's. I hope you found everything you needed," she said, walking up to a customer who had just been rang up. Then, she leaned over the counter and whispered to the ladies, "I need to talk to you all when you're done with the last of the customers waiting." They looked up one by one to let her know they had heard her and shook their head in the affirmative.

While she wait, Viviana went around to each register and counted the money inside them. Next, she placed more bills into the registers.

The staff was confused and wondered if something was wrong.

"What's going on," Sharon asked?"

The other three ladies stood around wanting to know the same. "Come on ladies, don't worry. It's nothing bad," Viviana assured them. Y'all can all relax," she added.

"Damn, Viv, don't scare us like that," Sandra said, playfully hitting her on the arm. My heart was racing so fast! I thought we messed up something while you were gone. Sandra held her chest as if her heart was going to jump through it.

"Everybody come into my office when we close. I was going to tell y'all now but I see we're still busy," she told them.

Viviana walked back to her office. She sat back down at her desk and decided to call Giovanni.

Seeing Viviana's name appear on his phone's screen, he quickly answered.

"Hello," he said into the phone.

"Hi, baby," Viviana replied. How's your day going, babe?" she asked naturally.

"Pretty good, baby. No complaints," he answered, "but even better now that you've called."

"Aww, baby. You so sweet. You always know just what to say to make me smile." As she held the phone she began to blush although Giovanni couldn't see her. "I feel the same way.... I just had to call 'cause I was missin' my boo." She sighed heavily.

"Well you already know I'm missin' yo' fine, sexy ass," Giovanni replied flirtatiously. "But where you at anyway," he asked.

"Oh, I'm down here at the store with the ladies tryna catch up on some paperwork," she explained, "and you?"

"I'm handling some business. You know me," he answered in that cocky way that turned her on.

"Yeah, I know you a busy man, baby, so I won't hold you for long," she said.

"Oh, don't rush, babe. You can call me whenever you want to," he told her.

"I know, babe," she smiled. "But there *is* something I was calling to ask you..." she paused momentarily, "I wanted to know if the jet is at the private airport. I was sitting here thinking about how hard the girls here have been working, and I thought it'd be nice to take them on a mini-vacation to show my appreciation," she informed him. "they have really been holdin' things down here at the store, babe."

Giovanni knew the kind of woman Viviana was, and she took her businesses serious. She had established a name for herself because of them and she was well respected by people all over the city. A business man himself, he knew it took dedicated, hard workers to run a business. He could understand why it was important to Viviana to reward her staff, and without hesitation, he told her so.

"Sure, babe, of course you can," he obliged. It's exactly where I told you it would be. I told you, you could use the jet anytime you wanted to. It belongs to both of us," he reminded her.

"Thank you, babe," she replied.

"Now let me get back to my business, Viv, so I can come home and handle more business," he replied and laughed. "I love you," he said before saying goodbye.

"I love you too, Giovanni. Talk to you later."

After hanging up with Giovanni, she sat daydreaming of being in his arms later that evening. Without realizing what she'd done, Viviana stuck her finger in her mouth and sucked it lightly. *Oh my God! I'm so in love with that man...*

Later that day…

Viviana made her rounds through the store, straightening items on the shelves, and checking to make sure all the registers had been locked for the day. Next, she pulled the gate that secured the store, halfway down. The only thing left for her to do was turn the lights off. Nonetheless, rather than turn them completely down to the off level, she only dimmed them partially.

"Y'all can follow me in my office," she said, gesturing the ladies to come with her. Once inside, she sat down at her desk like the BOSS she knew she was. The ladies went in behind her and sat down, wondering what this unexpected meeting was all about. One by one, they looked at Viviana curiously.

"So, ladies," she said. "I know you're all wondering why I had you come to my office." All the ladies shook their head up and down in agreement with her assumption.

"First, I wanna say I appreciate all of you, and all you have done for me and this store… I wouldn't have made it without any of you. I love you guys so much, truly I do. I have a loyal team who's been handling business since the day the doors of this store opened."

Viviana could feel herself getting emotional because everything she'd said was genuine and true. And the truth of the matter was, she wasn't always an easy person to work for, and her work ethic codes were strict. All the ladies knew she didn't play when it came to her business and her money. But even so, they had hung right by her side and worked hard every day.

"Because of your hard work and devotion, we're gonna ball out of control!" she yelled.

Still not understanding what she meant, the ladies looked at one another then back at Viviana.

"Ladies, to show my appreciation, I talked to Giovanni and he gave me the okay to take *all* of you to the Hamptons for the weekend, on our private jet!" she finally told them.

"Are you serious?" they asked one after the other.

"Hell yeah, I'm serious!" she laughed excitedly, "so y'all go home, and pack your bags for the weekend 'cause we 'bout to have some fun!"

She stood up and one of the girls screamed, "Yay!"

Another cried out and said, "Thank you, Viv! You the bomb!"

Everyone was ecstatic as they each took turns giving their boss a hug.

———————

When the end of the week came, Viviana closed the store an hour early. All the ladies had been excited and couldn't stop talking about the trip, and they were all set to leave for the Hamptons later that Friday evening.

It was 10 p.m. and Viviana had already boarded the jet at the Teterboro Airport for private planes. As she sat waiting for the ladies to arrive and board, she checked to make sure there were plenty of drinks on board.

Not long after, Sandra, Sharon, Liz, and Tonya, all boarded the jet together.

"Welcome, ladies," Viviana greeted them. "I hope you bitches are ready to kick it boss-style," she asks, pulling out some champagne flutes.

"Oh my God, Viv," Tonya said.

"This shit is fly as fuck," Sharon added.

"Girl, this is lovely," Liz told her.

"Thank you, girl," Viviana replied, handing them each a flute of Moët, and for the remained of the flight, the ladies kicked back and laughed over drinks, as they waited for the jet to prepare to land.

An hour and nine minutes later, they were landing, arriving at the Farmingdale Airport located in the Hamptons.

"Well Viv, that was a quick flight," Sharon said, just as she realized the jet had landed.

"Yeah, it really was," Viviana agreed. "Now that we're here though, I want us to enjoy our night before it gets too late since we'll be leaving Monday morning. That gives us the rest of tonight, along with Saturday and Sunday to have some fun," she explained.

After exiting the jet, Viviana led the way to the Mercedes truck limo she had arranged to be awaiting them.

"No, you didn't girl! Oh my God," Tonya said in awe of the limo.

"I told you guys I was gonna show my appreciation to you all," Viviana said as if the limo were an everyday thing.

"Cuzzie, this shit is so flyy!" Sandra said in a loud tone. She looked around and rubbed the seats, amazed at the custom made interior designing.

"So where are we headed to now?" Sharon asked her cousin.

"I rented a beach house for us and dinner should be waiting on us when we arrive," she answered.

"Good, Cuzzie 'cause I'm starving."

"Me too," everyone else echoed.

Viviana then told the ladies, "We all are gonna be hungry, because we still have to ride like another hour to get to the beach house."

"Aww man," Tonya said.

"Yep, I'm sorry ladies. There was no way I could get a plane to land out there because there's nothing but water surrounding the house.

"It's cool, Cuzzie, we understand," Sharon said.

Yeah, Viv, I'm cool with that too. I'm just so thankful you thought enough of us to bring us on this vacation," Sandra told her.

"Yeah, now we can get turned up," Liz said, throwing her hand in the air as she shakes her ass.

Everyone laughed at how silly she was acting. Viviana smiled and grabbing her cell phone from her purse. She dialed Giovanni's number but didn't get an answer. She hang up and dialed it again. *Damn my baby always picks up for me... I hope he's okay . . .* But again, no answer.

Viviana put her cell phone back inside her purse. *Oh well, he's probably busy,* she thought, *he'll call me back when he sees I called him . . .* She tried to get the unanswered call off her mind but something inside her just wouldn't allow her to do so. Not wanting to alarm the other ladies, she snaps her fingers and tries to enjoy the music playing through the Bose speakers of the limo.

Sharon, always the observant one, notices the worried look on Viviana's face. "Are you okay, Viv?" she asked in a concerned tone of voice.

"Yeah, girl… I'm fine," she answered with a halfhearted smile, and tried to enjoy the ride.

An hour later the limo pulled up to the Beach House.

"Whoa, Viv this is luxurious, I love it," Liz said, looking up at the Beach House.

"Oh, my goodness, you guys! Yeah, this is beautiful. I've never seen this place until now," Viviana said. I saw the pictures and the reviews online when I booked the place, but this is a beautiful sight," she said, admiring the beach house.

She opened the door so that everyone could get their bags and head inside.

"I'm telling everybody right now," Viviana shouted, "do not touch my room—the one with the all marble interior and fireplace!" "Actually, all the rooms have fireplaces but mine is the only one with the marble tile," she said. 'But, we'll get to that later. Anybody else starved besides me," she asked, rubbing her stomach for emphasis.

"I am," Tonya said.

"Me too," said Liz.

The girl's sat down at the Island Bar where there were all kinds of finger foods, veggies, and fruits. Viviana took a seat at the Island with the ladies and took a sip of her glass of lemon-water with before eating.

"Umm… everything tastes so good, huh ladies?" she asked.

"Oh God, yes!" Tonya replied.

"Your hungry-ass feel better now that you got some food in you?" Viv asked her.

"Heck yeah, girl," she answered as she piles her plate up a second time. "I don't care what y'all think of me. I'm starving," she said and shoved some pasta in her mouth.

After dinner, the ladies got comfortable in their pajamas. Sitting on the sectional sofa, they sipped Merlot, laughed, and enjoyed each other's company.

"So how is everyone enjoying themselves so far?" Viv asked. "Because I'm telling y'all, this is just the beginning! I know I'm enjoying myself," she told them.

"So am I," one of the ladies said.

"Me too," said another.

Soon, the wine kicked in and everyone was buzzed and feeling good. One by one, they got up from the sofa and started to dance. They laughed and gossiped and had a ball until the wee hours of the morning.

At some point, everyone had fallen asleep, but Viviana, however, had woken up in the middle of the night. Making her way to her, she realized Giovanni had never called her back. Now, she began to worry, and her stomach felt as though they had butterflies inside it; it wasn't like him not to call her back. Again, she dialed his number, and this time it went straight to his voicemail.

Oh God, Giovanni, where are you? I pray you're okay, she thought. She looked at her phone hoping it would suddenly ring. *I'm not gonna panic or jump to any conclusions because I know my baby loves me, and he wouldn't do anything he's not supposed to.* She laid the phone down on the bed, and before she knew it, she was sound asleep.

Saturday morning all the girls got up and met in the kitchen to have breakfast together. There was everything you could think of—fruits and bagels, omelets, and waffles, sausage, ham, bacon, the works!

Nibbling on strawberries, Viviana paced the floor as she continued to try and reach Giovanni. The ladies had noticed how she was acting and begin to wonder what had gotten her so seemingly distraught.

"Viv what's wrong?" Sharon questioned her.

"Nothin' Sharon," she said, "it's just that I've been trying to reach Giovanni ever since we arrived, but he hasn't answered nor returned any of my calls. At first, his phone was just ringing, but now, it's just going straight to his voicemail."

Viviana could no longer hide the fact that she was beginning to worry.

"I don't know, Sharon… that's not like him at all. He would have called me by now," she said, placing her phone on the counter.

She sat down at the Island and Sandra walked over to her and gently rubbed her back. "You don't think—

"No, Sandra! Don't even say it!"

She shook her head and hurried off to her room. Sitting on the edge of the bed with her coffee in her hand, she stared off in a silent daze.

Sharon and Sandra quickly went to her room to make sure she was okay. They sat beside her and tried to ease her mind.

"Viv, Cuzzie, you alright? I didn't mean to upset you," Sandra said.

"It's okay, Sandra. I'm fine, just a little concerned, that's all. I mean, come on y'all, it don't take a rocket scientist to figure out what Giovanni does, and I'm just starting to worry now."

Viviana's eyes became blurry as her tears threaten to fall. Sharon pulled her in close and allowed her head to rest on her shoulder. Sandra grabber her and squeezed it lightly, letting her know everything would be okay.

After the three of them hadn't come back to breakfast, Tonya and Liz finally went to find out what was going on with Viviana.

"Are you okay, Viv?"

"Yes, honey, I'm fine." She faked a smile and dried her eyes.

Viviana got up and went to get her luggage.

"Come on, let's go do some shopping!" she said, trying to change the mood.

4:00pm that afternoon

After taking the girls to Calypso St. to Barth's Boutiques, on a shopping adventure, Viviana took them to a store known as *Malia Mills,* a very high-class clothing store. Afterwards, they went to Tiffany & Co.

Viviana bought herself a diamond princess-cut tennis bracelet, with matching ring and watch, and bought Giovanni a pair of 8 carat diamond earrings and a Bulova watch with diamonds in the entire dial-face.

When they finished shopping, she treated them to a lovely dinner at an Italian restaurant called CittaNuova. After eating a wonderful dinner, we walked out of there looking like pregnant women, as we waddled to the limo.

Back at the beach house, Viviana showered and constantly thought about Giovanni. *I pray nothing is wrong.* After showering, she lotion her body and wished it could be Giovanni's hands rubbing on her bare skin.

Viviana couldn't sleep so she got up and decided to listen to some gospel music before watching TV. The mood she was in needed some inspiration and nothing seemed to inspire her like a powerful word from the gifted, spiritual, Bishop TD Jakes.

The gospel music from the TV must have woken the rest of the girls as Juanita Bynum's voice sang the words *I Don't Mind.* When the spiritual melody sounded from the television they came running in the room wanting to know what Viviana was watching.

She begin to tell them about Bishop TD Jakes and what a powerful speaker he was.

"He can preach that word for real," she said, as she lay down on the bed. "Why don't y'all come get up in this bed and watch him with me?" she suggested. She straightened up the covers of the bed, making a place for the girls to get comfortable.

"I've seen some of his sermons before," Sharon told Viv. "I'ma get some breakfast and coffee first, and then I'll come watch it with you.

"Fill my cup back up too, please," Viviana said, as she handed Sharon her cup.

Viviana's phone rang and to her surprise, it was Giovanni. She quickly answered the phone, anxious to hear his voice.

"Hello," she said, in a panicked tone.

"Hey babe," he replied. Giovanni sounded down.

"Giovanni… is everything alright?" she asked.

"Yes, baby doll, I'm okay, just missing you," he said sincerely.

"I miss you too, Giovanni baby."

"I can't wait to see you again," he said.

"Why haven't you been answering or returning my calls, babe?" she asked.

"Well, baby, the FEDS got me."

"What? Giovanni are you serious?" Viviana stood up and started pacing the floor.

"Yes, baby but I'm out now. I been locked up this whole damn time, babe," he told her.

"Aww damn, babe, I knew it. I knew something wasn't right. It's just not like you not to call me or return my calls." Viviana was happy he was out, but still, she needed to know what had happened.

"I'm sorry, my love," Giovanni said. "I'll make it up to you."

"No, Giovanni I'm just glad you're alright," she said, on the verge of tears. "I love you, baby."

"I love you so much, too," he reiterated. "I couldn't stop thinking about you while they had my ass locked up. I was sick not being able to talk to you."

"Yeah, me too, Giovanni. I was sick without you too, babe, I wish you were here with me."

"I wish I was there, too Viv, but you go enjoy the rest of your day with the girls and I'll holla at you later. I'ma go wash my ass and find out who set me up."

"Okay, baby, yeah handle your business but be careful,' Viviana told him.

"I will you, Viv."

"I'll make some phone calls too," she offered.

"No, Viv. You go enjoy yourself. I got this. I wasn't a hitman for nothin'. I'll find out sooner than later, ya heard." he said coolly. "By the way, when are y'all comin' back?" he asked curiously.

"We'll be leaving at 6 in the morning, but we probably won't get back until late morning," she replied.

"Ok, baby. I love you and I'll see you when you get back," Giovanni concluded.

"I love you more, and I can't wait to see you, me too babe, I'll call you a little later, bae, Ok boo love you and they hang up!

Talking to Giovanni had been such a relief for Viviana. The mere thought of something happening to him had almost put a damper on the remainder of the trip. But now, the question lingering in her mind was who could've possibly set him up, and why.

Both, Giovanni, and Viviana knew the FEDS were nothing to play with and being on their radar could cause big trouble. But for now, she would enjoy the little time she had left in the Hamptons, but best believe, she was going to get to the bottom of Giovanni's sudden run-in with the law, and somebody was going to pay...

═══════════

The sun was shining brightly, and the ladies sat by the pool, lounging, and having mixed drinks. Viviana drank grape juice because she didn't believe in drinking on Sundays.

"So, is everybody having a good time?" she asked.

"Oh, definitely," Liz answered.

"You know it," Tonya said.

"Hell yeah," Sharon replied.

"You ain't even gotta ask me," Sandra said and laughed, as she took a sip of her piña colada daiquiri.

The ladies thanked Viviana over and over again, they were all so appreciative she had done this for them. Tonight would be their last night and they would be heading back home the following day. Viviana hadn't yet decided if the store would open or remain closed; she thought giving the ladies an extra day to spend time with their families would be an added bonus to top off the trip.

I'm so ready to get back home," Sandra said. I'm just ready to sleep in my own bed."

"Who you telling, girl," Liz said, adding her two-cents. "I mean, don't get me wrong, this place is beautiful, but you know there's nothin' like home sweet own home."

"Yes, honey," Sharon said, "and laying up next to your man."

"Lord, I can't wait to get home to mine," Viviana told the girls. For a moment, she thought about Giovanni's encounter with the FEDS, but quickly pushed the thoughts out of her mind.

"Speaking of your man, have you heard from Giovanni?" Sharon asked.

"Yeah, he straight," Viviana answered curtly. We'll talk about that later though."

CHAPTER 11

"I'm so glad to be back on this plane headed back home," Viv stated.

"Yeah, me too, Viv," Sharon agreed, as she reclined her seat.

"Well, we should be landing in New Jersey in about a half an hour," Tonya said, looking at her wrist watch.

"Yeah, you're right, Tonya," Liz concurred. She yawned and stretched as she looked at the clouds from the window of the jet. "I tell ya' what," she added, "I ain't never been so happy to see Jersey in my entire life."

At Liz's remark, they all laughed and high-fived one another.

"But on a serious note, we'll probably be really busy on Tuesday since we're not opening up today," Viviana said.

"Yeah, I'm sure the customers will be coming through strong," said Sharon.

"Right, so you ladies better get home, get some rest, and be ready for the crowd in the morning," Viviana warned them.

Just as Tonya had predicted, the jet landed at the New Jersey Teterboro's Airport 30 minutes later. When they walked off the jet, just like in the Hamptons, Viviana had a limo and driver awaiting them to take them home.

"New Jersey, we're back!!!" Viviana yelled. They all laughed at her humor. "The first thing I'm gonna do when I get home is shower, and then I'm calling my man to come rub my back and give me a nice massage. And, of course, I'll give him one as well," she laughed and winked at the girls deviously.

"You so nasty, Viv." Liz looked at her and gave her the 'stank face'.

Viviana rubbed it in even more and put her finger in her mouth, then she sucked it hard and pulled it back out, causing it to make a popping sound. The ladies laughed hysterically as they piled inside the limo and pulled off, headed home.

Viviana was the last one to get dropped off. After she exited the car, the driver carried her bags to the door. She reached in her bag and handed him a five-hundred-dollar tip after he'd sat the luggage at her door.

"Thank you, Sir," she said.

"It's been my pleasure to service to you," he told Viviana, refusing the money she was giving him. "My only pay is you letting Mr. Lucus know that I took care of you and your friends.

She looked at the driver, her facial expression, seemingly shocked. *Now how the hell the driver know Giovanni is my man*, she wondered... *oh well...* She picked up her bags and took them up the stairs.

She threw all her bags to the floor and plopped her tired body down on the edge of her bed. Next, she pulled out her phone and dialed Giovanni's number.

"What's up, babe," he answered on the second ring.

"Hi, baby." she said. "I miss you."

"I miss you too, Viv, and I'm so glad you made it home safely."

"Yes, baby, I did. God was surely watching over us the entire time we were away.

"Yes, nobody but God, Viv. He's always watching over us," he replied.

"Oh, before I forget, the limo driver told me to tell you that he took good care of me... what is that about?" she asked.

"Oh yeah. His name is Mr. Charles and he's been my driver for a long time now," Giovanni informed her.

"Oh, I see. Well, I'm about to get in the shower and I'll be over to see you when I get out," she told him.

"I can't wait to see you. I'ma make some good lovin' to you, girl," he told her, causing his soldier to rise.

"Mmm, babe, Giovanni stop… Let me get there before you start turning me on," she cooed.

"Well you just hurry yo sexy ass up," he replied.

"Bye boi," she said, smiling. "Oh, babe, wait," she called out before he could hang up. "I forgot to tell you I got you something while we were in the Hamptons."

"Baby you didn't have to do that," he said modestly.

"I know, but I did, so too late now. Bye, boo, see you in a few." She made kissing sounds into the phone's receiver and disconnected the call.

Viviana undressed and made her way to the bathroom. Giovanni always made her feel sexy no matter what was going on and she could hardly wait to be in his arms again.

Just as she was about to step into the shower a thought crossed her mind. She ran back out of the bathroom, grabbed her phone, and sent a quick text:

Viv: babe I'm gonna make u 4get about all the time you spent behind those bars xoxox

Then she hit the send key.

Giovanni was just about to freshen up when the sound of Kem's *I Can't Stop Loving You*, began playing on his phone letting him know he had an incoming text from Viviana. He picked up the phone and opened the message:

Viv: babe I'm gonna make u 4get about all the time you spent behind those bars xoxox

As he read the text a huge smile spread across his face and he could feel the tingle inside his boxers. He closed the phone and shook his head from side to side. *Lord, that girl is something else…*

Later that day, Viviana and Giovanni lay in bed together at his penthouse. The two had made love repeatedly after she had arrived. They had missed each other tremendously and one couldn't get enough of the other.

Viviana rolled off Giovanni as she tried to catch her breathe.

"Whew-weee! Girl, I'ma need an oxygen mask puttin' in work like that!" he teased.

"Boy, you are crazy," Viviana said, as she playfully popped him on the head. She kissed his lips and lay her head against his hard chest. "Baby," she said, "I want you to come to the store with me tomorrow."

Her request had taken Giovanni by surprise, but he would do anything for her, and besides, it was no big deal.

"Okay, that's cool. Anything you want, you got it. Yeah, I'll go for sure," he answered. "But for now, let me get back into this good pussy," he said and quickly flipped her on her back. "Mmm," he moaned.

As he kissed and sucked on her nipples, it drove Viviana crazy.

"Oh God, Giovanni I love the way you suck on my nipples… oh God, baby, ummm…

When he entered inside her and began with slow, easy strokes, it felt so good, she grabbed him by his ass cheeks and pulled him in deeper, as she began to match him stroke-for-stroke.

"Ooh… damn, Viviana…' he whispered in her ear. "Damn, baby… you feel so good, I don't ever wanna stop."

When Viviana began nibbling and sucking on his neck, the soft touch of her lips sent chills through his body, causing him to push deeper inside her. He picked up the speed and began pounding her faster and harder. She arched her back and dug her nails into his waist as she held on for dear life.

The room was quiet and all that could be heard was the sounds of their love-making. The bed rocked and squeaked, and the headboard hit up against the wall so loud, she was sure the neighbors knew his name.

"Oh my God, Giovanni!" she cried out. "Giovanni, baby, I love you!"

At the sound of Viviana calling his name so passionately, Giovanni exploded and released himself deep inside her womb, and just seconds after, her own fireworks went off.

While looking into one another's eyes as if in a daze, it was evident the love between them had grown in just a short amount of time.

When he'd drained her totally dry, he pulled her into his arms and kissed her on every part of her face before saying, "I love you," and not long after, they had dozed off happy, satisfied, and content.

A few hours later, they woke up and neither was ready to get out of bed. While lying in bed, they played, laughed, and talked about their future together.

Viviana looked at Giovanni with a childish grin. "Baby," she said, "we have to stop all these sexual rendezvous before I end up pregnant," she told him playfully, as she lay propped up on her elbow facing him.

"I would love to have my first child with the lady I want to spend the rest of my life with. Haven't you noticed I never pull out when I reach that point? There's a reason for that, babe. I know exactly what I'm doing." He laughed.

"So, let me get this straight," she sat up in bed, "you're *trying* to get me pregnant?" she asked a bit surprised.

"You damn right I am. Girl I'm trying to put my seeds all up inside of you," he said. He leaned down and kissed her on her stomach.

"Oh, wow. I never paid it any mind, although I should have," she admitted. "For real though, I would love to have a child one day. It would be a blessing to have a son or a daughter. Just as long as it's healthy, I'd be the happiest woman on earth," Viviana replied. She rubbed the top of Giovanni's head as he continued to plant kisses all over her stomach.

"Yeah a boy or a girl. It doesn't really matter to me," he said in agreement. "With you as the baby's mommy, I know he or she will be beautiful."

The two became quiet, each lost in their own thoughts. Giovanni daydreamed about having a son, and Viviana wondered if they really would have a child together, especially given the recent events. Changing the subject to something that had been weighing heavily on her mind, Viviana decided to get it off of her chest.

"Baby," she began, "did you ever find out who set you up?"

Giovanni sighed and looked away. The thought of being locked up made him angry, and not knowing who was responsible made him even angrier.

"Nah, babe, but I will. Trust me," he said. The anger resonated in his tone. That was a side he tried to hide from Viviana. "I gotta lot of people out there looking for answers, so I know I'll find out soon, babe."

Viviana couldn't hold back the tears that had welled up in her eyes. When Giovanni felt the wetness on his chest, he sat up and looked at her seriously.

"What's wrong, baby?" he asked as he held her in his arms and rocked her gently.

"I just get so worried about you baby," she said softly.

He touched her face and wiped her tears away and told her not to worry. "I'll be fine, just trust me. Stop worrying," he repeated. "Look, baby I promise you this won't happen again," he assured her. "I love you, Viviana, and I'm not gonna let nothin' happen to either of us, that's a promise," he vowed. "I'll go to my grave trying to protect you, girl... I love you and I will kill a muthafucka that tries to stand in my way. You're my heart Viviana Lucus."

"I love you too, Giovanni."

CHAPTER 12

Viviana walked into Belladonna's and the staff stood at their usual registers, ringing up customers as usual. However, something in the atmosphere seemed solemn. The ladies didn't have their usual enthusiasm and their smiles appeared strained and forced.

She noticed immediately but figured the recent trip had given them jet lag, or perhaps they were still tired from all the weekend activities. Walking to her office, she was still a bit tired herself; however, as soon as she turned to close the office door, Sandra and Sharon rushed in behind her; the looks on their faces was one she had never seen before, and she knew something was wrong.

"We have to talk, Viv," Sharon told her as soon as the door closed behind them.

Viviana sat down at her desk and reached for her morning cup of coffee. "What's going on? Why are you looking like that?" Viviana's voice was laced with concern.

"Viv, this is very serious," Sandra said.

"What is it?" Viviana asked again in a louder tone. She sat her coffee back down on her desk and looked at her cousins, waiting for an answer.

Sandra and Sharon hesitated, afraid of what might be going on. They loved their cousin as if she were their sister and they knew the business she was in could one day turn ugly for her.

"Do you want to tell her, or do you want me to tell her?" Sandra asked her sister.

"Tell me what," Viviana asked again with a frown on her face. "Stop beating around the damn bush and say what it is you have to say," she demanded of her cousins. "Did somebody steal from me?" she asked, with a look of anger.

"No, Viv," Sandra said. "Look, Viv. I'ma keep it all the way real with you 'cause ain't no easy way to tell you this shit," she said before continuing. "Some dudes came in the store looking around, asking about you and everything," she finally told her.

"Okay, and?" Viviana replied, "go on. What they look like?"

"Some white dudes dressed in casual clothing, nothing major," Sharon explained further. "But me and Sandra knew exactly who they were when they walked in the door."

"The muthafuckin' FEDS," both women said, nearly in unison.

"Damn," Viviana said, shaking her head from side to side. "Ain't this about a bitch." She jumped up from her seated position at the desk and banged her fist on the wall angrily. "Did they try and talk to Toya or Liz?" she asked calmly. She looked at them intensely, listening to their every word.

"No, Viv. We stopped them before they had the chance to," said Sandra.

"Oh my God, what the hell is going on?" she asked no one in particular, "first Giovanni gets set up and hauled to jail, now the fucking FEDS coming to my place of business asking questions about me. It's a fuckin' rat somewhere around this camp, I ain't no damn fool and I know the damn game too well," she said in tone she rarely used. "This shit cannot be fuckin' happening right now! Somebody punk-ass is snitchin'!"

"Straight like that, Cuzzie," Sharon said, meaning she agreed one-hundred percent. "That's the same damn thing I said, Viv."

"Well, one thing for certain, and two for sure," Viviana said with a vicious look in her eyes. "You and me both know what happens to bitch-ass snitches—

Before she could complete her thought, Sandra reached down in her left sock, and pulled her 9mm out and cocked it with a quickness that said she wasn't new to this.

She looked at her sister then back at Viv. This what the fuck happens," she said. "What? Niggas thought we was playin'? Yeah, okay,"

"They about to learn the hard way," Sharon added. "Try not to worry, Viv. We gonna get to the bottom of this shit real quick."

The sisters leaned in and gave Viviana a hug and kissed her on the cheek. They walked to the door preparing to go back out front. Just before they made their exit, Sandra looked over her shoulder at Viviana and said, "We got you, Cuzzie, and we ain't gonna stop until we find out who it is."

Viviana reached inside the desk drawer and held up her Glock-9. "That's if I don't find the muthafucka first," she said, slamming the gun down on the desk with a bang.

When she was alone in her office, she began scrolling through her mental rolodex. *These bitch ass snitches done set my baby up, got the FEDS coming around my fuckin' store and shit... These fools crazy... Do they really know who they messing with? This my fuckin' Empire they're interfering with.* Question after question and thought after thought raced through her mind. Somebody had messed up big time, and now, they had to pay.

Moments later, she had finally calmed down enough to call Giovanni.

"Hey, babe what's up?" he asked, greeting her in his usual manner. "How is your morning going so far?"

Viviana had allowed her thoughts to drift off once again, and briefly, there was nothing but silence between the two.

"Hello?" Giovanni said, as he moved the phone away from his ear. He looked at the screen to make sure the call hadn't been dropped. "Viv, you there?"

"Oh, I'm sorry, babe. Yes, I'm still here; I'm just pissed right now," she told him.

Giovanni had been driving when she called, but hearing the dismay and anger in her voice, caused him to pull over and give her his undivided attention.

"What's wrong, baby? Tell me," he said in a demanding tone.

"When I got to work this morning, I walked in and the girls were looking kind of strange, so I asked what was wrong," she began explaining.

"Go 'head, I'm listenin'," he urged.

"So, Sandra and Sharon come in my office and—

"Those are your cousins, right?" Giovanni asked, cutting her off midsentence.

"Yes, baby, but listen. Long story short, they told me the muthafuckin'' FEDS came in my store looking around and asking them all kinds of questions about me and shit. Shit is crazy." she said, recalling what she'd been told.

"What the fuck?" The information Viv had given Gio caused him to look around him. Now, he was paranoid of being followed.

"Listen, I want to meet you somewhere. I'm leaving the store right now, and I'll call you as soon as I get inside my car," Viviana said.

"I love you, Viv," Gio said, ending the conversation.

"Love you too," she replied, right before the lines disconnected.

Viviana grabbed her bag and keys and rushed out front to let the staff know she was leaving. Tonya and Liz knew it was unlike her to leave so suddenly, especially since she'd just gotten there.

"Is everything okay, Viv?" Liz asked.

"Just fine," she answered curtly. "I just need you all to hold things down until I come back."

"We got it covered," Liz assured her.

"Thanks, ladies," she said. "I'll keep you posted," she said looking toward Sharon and Sandra as she exited the store.

Viviana walked briskly to her car and hopped in. She needed to call Giovanni but felt it might not be safe to use her cell phone. Being that the FEDS were hot on her trail, they could have easily had her phone traced by now. Contemplating on what to do, she decided to use her car phone instead. She dialed his number and he answered on the first ring.

"Viv, you alright, baby," he asked.

"Hey, babe. I'm fine," she said. "I'm using my car phone because the Feds may have a trace on my cell phone."

"Good thinking baby. So, where do you want to meet?" he asked.

"Meet me at 560 Mable St. Southside New Jersey at my deli."

"Alright, I'm on it," he told her.

"See you in a few," Viviana said and quickly ended the call.

Viviana walked inside the deli and hugged her cousins. Giovanni had been sitting outside waiting when she arrived, and he walked in behind her.

"Who is this fine ass man behind you?" Martha asked.

Might I ask the same?" Gloria chimed in, as she leaned over the counter to shake Giovanni's hand.

"This is my fiancé I was telling you both about," Viviana said.

"He's a good look on you," Martha said with a smile.

After the brief introductions had been made, Viviana and Giovanni went to Viviana's office where they could talk in private.

"What's up, babe?" Giovanni asked as Viviana seated herself at one of the booth's in the deli. "This a nice little deli you got here, Viv."

"Thank you, babe," she said.

"Now what's the deal?" Giovanni asked, getting straight to business.

"I don't know what the hell is going on. I just know it can't be a coincidence that you got locked up, and now all of a sudden the FEDS are snoopin' around my place of business. This shit just don't seem right," Viviana said, speaking in a soft tone as not to be overheard.

Giovanni reached across the table and held her hand.

"Look at me, Viv," he said. "I told you, I promised your father I would take care of you, and, because of that promise, I would die for you, baby. I would die to keep his empire alive," he said seriously. "You hear me, Viv?"

Viviana looked down because she didn't want him to see the fear in her eyes. Giovanni noticed and placed his finger underneath her chin, using it to guide her focus back to his eyes.

"Do you hear me?" he asked again.

"Yes, Giovanni. I do, babe. I just don't want this to turn into a blood-bath."

"If that's what it's gotta be, then that's what it's *gonna* be, babe," he stressed.

"I hear you, babe, and believe me, ain't nothin' soft about me either. I'ma boss bitch. Down for whatever. My father taught me to fear no man," she replied. "The only thing that scares me is the thought of losing everything he worked so hard for. My daddy died in the game," she said proudly.

"It's on then," Gio said. "I got this." The look in his eyes reflected that of a killer, and even Viviana was unaware of the levels to his viciousness; however, she would soon find out.

Gloria and Martha walked over to them and sat down next to Viviana. "Is everything good over here?" Gloria asked.

Viviana looked at Giovanni then back at Martha and Gloria. Noticing her hesitation to answer, Giovanni shook his head, giving her the okay.

"Well… last weekend I took the staff of Belladonna's to the Hamptons to show my appreciation of their hard work." Pausing, she ran her fingers through her hair and let out a heavy sigh.

"While we were in the Hamptons," she continued, "Giovanni got set up and ended up going to jail." At the mention of that, Giovanni scratched his head, unsure of the reaction he would get from Martha and Gloria.

"What?" Gloria yelled out.

Viviana reached over and rubbed his face lovingly. "See, unbeknownst to me, Giovanni worked for my father for a long time before I ever knew who he was."

Martha and Gloria stared at Giovanni intensely and said nothing. At first sight, something about him had seemed familiar but neither could recall where they had seen or heard of him. Then, as if a light bulb had suddenly gone off, Gloria snapped her finger and said, "So, you must be Uncle Ricardo's hitman?"

Viviana and Giovanni looked at one another, both wearing stunned expressions. "Gloria how do you know that?" he asked.

"I've heard a lot about you, and I'm very pleased to finally meet the man my cousin has placed so much trust into," she told him.

"Welcome to the family," Martha added. "So, Viv, this must be serious."

"Yes, Martha, but don't worry," Viv said. "We just need a few days to find out who is after us.

"If you know anything about me, you also know my reach is far, and finding people is what I do," Giovanni said, as he leaned on the table.

"I worked for Ricardo for many years, but I started with very little experience. He took a chance on me and taught me everything I know. "I know the ends and outs to this game and muthafuckas who snitch eventually disappear." He said full of confidence.

"But wait, there's more," Viviana told them. "When I got to work at the store this morning, Sharon and Sandra came in my office tellin' me the damn FEDS been to *my* damn place askin' questions and shit. It's a good thing me and Giovanni slept in this morning, which made me late, otherwise they would've probably hauled my ass to jail for questioning."

"What the fuck, Viv? Oh, hell nah, this shit is mad weird," Gloria said. Giovanni got locked up, now the FEDS goin' to your store? Something foul is definitely goin' on."

"I agree," Martha said, "shit ain't right."

"Yeah, I know, but shit 'bout to get real 'round this bitch now," Viviana said convincingly.

"'I'll get the bottom of who it is and put an end to this shit." Giovanni said, as he got up and walked out of the deli.

"Giovanni!" Viviana called after him, nevertheless, he kept walking and didn't bother to look back. She jumped up and started to go after him.

Martha stopped her and said, "Girl just let him be, he'll be alright. He's upset right now, and for good reasons."

"That nigga right there," Gloria said, pointing in Giovanni's direction, "is a straight killer," she informed them. "I heard about that maniac, and I feel for the person who is trying to bring you down. No, I take that back," she thought aloud, "as a matter of fact, he need to murder them pussies," and with that said, Gloria stood and walked away.

"Damn right," Martha agreed, as she too, stood up from the table. "Viv, shit is crazy and we're gonna keep our eyes and ears open, but in the meantime, you really need to stay away from the store for a while. "Now that you know they are watching you."

"You're right Martha and I have considered working from home for a few weeks. I don't know what I will tell Tonya and Liz though," Viviana said. "Sharon and Sandra already know what time it is."

"Shit tell 'em you have to be away from the store for a while." Gloria suggested, "overseas handling some business or something…

shit, you the boss, you don't have to answer to anyone but yourself." Gloria said, as she went back behind the counter to help Martha.

———————

Tonya answered the phone, "Hello, thank you for calling Belladonna's. How can I help you?"

"Tonya?"

"Yes, Viv? It's me.

"How's everything going over there?" Viv asked.

"It's good, been steady. We had a little crowd, but we put in team work and got it cleared out pretty quickly."

"Well, good that's what I like to hear. So, I was calling to tell you guys that I'll be going out of the country for a few days to handle some business pertaining to the store. Actually, I have to take a few business trips," she lied. "Tell the girls and make sure you tell Sharon and Sandra."

"Okay, Viv, I will.

Viviana hung up and thought to herself, *what next*...

CHAPTER 13

Giovanni and Viviana decided to drive to Giovanni's parents' Estate. Viviana looked out the window in amazement as they drove down the long narrow driveway. There were giant Dahlias of red and white on each side of the driveway. She was beginning to think they were on a golf course, until she finally saw an opening that revealed a high pond with beautiful white swans floating freely on top of the beautiful water.

Viviana was even more astonished when she saw the humongous Victorian house sitting across the pond. It looked like a picture straight out of the Hamptons. Giovanni got out of the car and walked around to her side to open the door for her.

As they walked up the pathway to his parent's grand wood door, he yelled for his parents.

"Yes, son. I'm here," his mother said, as she made her way to the formal dining room area where he and Viviana had seated themselves. Mrs. Lucus was a vision of sassy beauty. She was average height, with short tapered hair and not a piece out of place. Her complexion was that of light caramel. She wore a simple, yet elegant sundress of many bright colors that seemed to make her skin glow even brighter.

"Hi, Mom," he said and hugged and kissed his mother, "this is Viviana, your soon to be daughter in law."

"Hello, Mrs. Lucus. It's such an honor to meet you." she reached out and hugged Giovanni's mother.

"Sweetie, it's my pleasure to meet you as well," Mrs. Lucus replied. "And please, call me Evett dear."

She took Viviana by the hand and led the way to introduce her to Giovanni's father. Giovanni followed behind them.

"Mom, where is my pops?"

"You know your father is in his man-cave," Mrs. Lucus said as she looked back at Giovanni.

"Oh yeah, where he always is." Giovanni laughed. He knew his father well.

"Giovanni, baby, she's a very beautiful lady," Mrs. Lucas complimented.

"Thank you, Ms. Evett," Viviana said as she blushed.

"Yes, Mom, she is, and I love her so much." Giovanni kissed Viviana and popped her on her butt.

"Stop boy." Viviana pushed Giovanni away, "see how he do me Mrs. Evett?"

"He's just like his father, baby. Get used to it," she said, as she smiled at Viviana.

"Yes hun, your man and my husband are some major freaks."

"Mom, really?" Giovanni said, slightly embarrassed.

"Oh my God, Ms. Evett, you're a mess."

"No, baby, I'm serious. You've got a freak on your hands, just like his father." They all laughed.

"Okay, baby, come on down here," Mrs. Evett said, leading them down the stairs to Mr. Johnny's man-cave.

Johnny looked up, "Who's here, baby?"

"It's your son and future daughter-in-law!"

"Hey, Pops! How you been?" Giovanni said, giving his father a dap on the hand.

"I've been cool, Son. Enjoying this life, and enjoying retirement with your mother, with her fine ass."

They all laughed, and Mrs. Evett winked at Viviana, "See, I told you… a freak to his name!"

"Look at this gorgeous one right here," Mr. Johnny said, as he stood up to greet Viviana, "give your future daddy a hug."

"Hello, Mr. Lucus." Viviana moved in close and gave Mr. Lucas a warm embrace.

"She's beautiful son."

"Yes, she is dad… this my baby right here. She's the prettiest woman in the world aside from Mom," Giovanni said, holding Viviana next to him.

Mr. Johnny and Mrs. Evett looked at them and smiled brightly.

"Thank you, Mr. Lucus," Viviana said.

"You all have a lovely home here. It's simply beautiful!"

"Well thank you, baby," Mr. Lucas replied, "and call me Johnny, pretty lady. But, you never told me your name."

"Oh, damn, I'm sorry, Dad. This is Viviana," Giovanni said, formally introducing them.

"A beautiful name for a beautiful person." Mr. Lucas winked playfully at Viviana.

"Thank you, Mr. Johnny," she said shyly.

"Are you guy's hungry?" he asked.

"Yes, I'm starving." Viviana rubbed her stomach and hoped he hadn't heard it growl.

"Me too, Dad."

"Well, come on, Son, let's you and me start this grill up! Baby, you and my little cutie of a daughter in law can go hit the kitchen," Mr. Johnny said, hinting to the women to get upstairs.

Viviana kissed Giovanni. "Your parents are a mess."

"Yes, bae, this I know. But you ain't seen nothin' yet."

"I love you, Giovanni."

"I love you too, Viv."

―――――――――

"Umm! This grilled shrimp and lobster is so good."

"Thank you, Viviana."

"You and my baby did y'all thang on the grill."

"You did your thang with this broccoli casserole too. It's to die for. You've gotta give me this recipe, Mrs. Evett said.

"Yes, of course. The recipe is very simple," Viviana told her, "but I got you." She looked over and smiled at Giovanni's mother.

"You put your foot in this for sure." They all laughed.

"Thanks everyone," she said.

"Yes, Dad, my baby can cook. Matter of fact, she *loves* to cook."

"I sure do, Mr. Johnny," Viviana replied.

"She's trying to fatten me up Mom and Dad."

"Yeah, Son, I see. You've gained a few pounds since the last time I saw you." Mr. Lucas playfully tapped his son on the belly.

"Yeah, Son, you have picked up a few pounds lately," Mrs. Evett agreed, as she put some of the lobster in her mouth.

"He looks good to me though," Viviana added and kissed Giovanni on the cheek.

"Thank you, babe." He kissed Viviana back.

Later that night, Gio and Viv sat by the pool, sipping on some wine, taking in the night air. The landscaping in his parents' backyard was beautiful. The view was just lovely.

"Oh, Giovanni, it's so beautiful out here. We should buy us a house out here, baby."

"My parents really do have great taste." He leaned in and kissed Viv passionately as if he wanted to make love to her right then and there.

"Umm. . . Stop, Giovanni," she whined as he kissed her on her neck. "Umm… that feels good baby. Stop before things get out of hand out here. You don't want your parents to find me out here riding you like a mechanical bull." They both started to laugh.

Giovanni looked deep into Viviana's eyes and kissed her again. You are so pretty, Viv. I want to have a daughter who looks just like you, babe," he said. Give me a daughter. I want to take you now and cum inside you until I get my daughter."

Viviana looked at him and saw the love he held for her. "I love you too, baby. You're everything a woman could want in a man. I would be proud to have a son who's a complete replica of you."

"Fine with me, Viv. Let's make love right now. Let's go inside the house so we can work on making some kids," he said grabbing her by the hand.

"Let's go baby," Viviana said as she got up. "Oh, does your mom have any grapefruits in the kitchen?" Giovanni looked at Viviana knowingly. I think I may be able to find some.

She kissed him and they both went inside the house laughing and fondling one another.

"Let's go say goodnight to your parents," Viviana said, as she looked at Giovanni getting out of the shower.

"Alright hold on. Let me put some shorts on. Grabbing a pair of his Gucci boxers, Viviana went over and got on her knees, and began sucking his manhood so good, Giovanni put his hands on her head and leaned back.

"Ohh, Viv, suck this dick girl… you sucking this like you want some more of it damn, girl…"

"You like it?" she asked, looking up at Giovanni.

"Yes, I love it, Viv, umm… You want this dick, baby?"

"Yes, Giovanni, I want it now."

Giovanni picked her up from the floor, took her robe off and began to suck on her nipples.

"It turns me on when you suck on my nipples like that, baby, damn!"

He stuck his finger inside her wetness and she stopped him suddenly. Viviana knew if they ever got started, they would never go tell his parents goodnight.

"Stop, Giovanni, stop, baby. We need to go tell your parents goodnight."

She kissed him on his head, and he continued to suck on her breasts.

"Oh, God, Giovanni, stop, baby."

———————

After telling his parents goodnight, Giovanni and Viviana lay in bed talking.

"Giovanni, who do you think is trying to destroy us, babe?"

Giovanni rubbed his chin as if he were deep in thought. "I don't know, bae, I really have no idea," he said truthfully, "but let's not talk about that right now. I just don't wanna spoil the mood," he told her.

He rubbed her on her stomach and rolled on top of her with ease. "Now let's make this baby," he whispered.

Again, he kissed Viviana on her lips. Slowly, he moved down her body like a snake slithering through the grass. When his lips brushed against her stomach, she grabbed him by the top of his head, and spread her legs to welcome him.

"I want lots of babies from you, Giovanni," she said in a soft voice. "Please, baby, make love to me and then fuck me," she said.

Giovanni took that as his queue. He loved driving her crazy, and he knew teasing her always did it. He slowly guided himself to her opening, only allowing the head to dip inside. When she tried to pull him in deeper, he pulled back out. Next, he moved back down and kissed her wetness before sticking his tongue inside and wiggling it around. Viviana almost lost it.

"Baby, now… please, I need to feel you inside me now," she pleaded.

Obeying her command, he climbed back on top of her and pushed his dick inside her slow, and easy yet deeply. In and out, in and out. Just as she started to throw it back, he pulled out again. This time, she cried out.

"Oh shit, yo dick-play is fire, babe!" she said loud enough for anyone in the house to hear her. Giovanni muffled her cries with a deep, passionate kiss, inviting her tongue to tango with his.

As he kissed her deeply, he pushed back inside her once more, but this time, it was game time. By now, Viviana's pussy was so sloppy wet, it began talking. As Giovanni rammed his dick in and out without mercy, the sounds of her wetness sounded like children running through rain puddles in Galoshes. The sound of their love making only intensified Giovanni's relentlessness to plant a seed inside her.

When Viviana's moans became louder, Giovanni stuck one of his fingers in her mouth, and she sucked on it greedily. She lifted her hips frantically, throwing the pussy back at him just the way he loved it. Pound for pound, stroke by stroke, they got closer and closer to that place of pure ecstasy.

"Viviana, baby, I will kill you if you ever fuck around on me," he whispered. "We would have to die together, baby," he said, breathlessly. "'Cause, I-I," he stuttered as he panted for air, "can't live wi-wi-without y-you," he said softly in her ear.

"I feel the same way, babe," she whispered back.

Her words sent him over the edge, causing him to place his hand around her neck, and hold it with a firm grip. Then, he began fucking her fast and hard, and then even harder. The sounds of his balls hitting her against her ass got louder and louder.

"Babe," she cried out. "I'm- I-I'm cumin'... Sss, ohh... Umm..." she moaned as her pussy began to skeet.

"I'm right be-be-behind you," Giovanni hissed as he exploded.

Viviana talked on the phone with Giovanni and she laughed hysterically. "Okay, babe, go ahead and handle your business, boo."

"Okay, love. I'll talk to you later," he said.

After speaking with him Viviana always felt better. No matter what was going on, he always seemed to make her smile.

Laying back on her bed, she thought about the wonderful time she'd had at his parents' house. *Mrs. Lucas is a trip,* she thought, *and Giovanni is definitely his father's son… they just alike.* She smiled at the thought. The sound of her phone ringing took her out of her reverie. *Damn there goes my phone again…*

"Hello," she answered.

"What's up stranger?" It was Felix.

"Hey, boy. What you been up to?" She smiled, happy to hear his voice.

"Nothin' much," he said, "same ole same ole; still grindin' hard, and fuckin' with these broads."

Viviana laughed. "Boy, you better be careful out here with these skanks. I hope you stayin' strapped up."

"Hell, yeah I stay trapped up. I just let these hoes suck my dick." he said with a chuckle.

"Oh my God, boy you crazy and nasty as hell," she laughed again. "But how've you been, Cuz?" he asked.

"I've been fine. You know neither one of us can sit still for long."

"True." She agreed.

"Well, Viv, I was just callin' to check on you," he told her.

"Okay, Felix. Thanks, I appreciate that, but let's get together and have some dinner sometime soon," she suggested.

"Okay, sounds good to me," he said accepting the invitation.

"On you right?" Viv asked.

Felix laughed, "Yeah, Cuz, you got that fo' sho."

"Alright then, Viv, let me know when. I'll holla at you," he said before hanging up.

Viviana laid back down and decided to call her mother. It had been a while since they'd last talked and she missed her. She hit the speed dial she had assigned to her mom and let the phone ring.

Paula picked up. "Hello."

"Hey, Mama."

"Hey, Viviana. How you been, baby?"

"I've been good, Mama. Everything been okay with you?"

"Yes, baby, I'm doing good."

"Well good, Mama. I know I haven't called you in a while, so I wanted to call and see how you've been."

"I know you're a busy woman, Viv, and I know you have your own life to live, so it's okay, baby."

"Thanks, Ma."

"Don't worry about Mama. Mama is just fine. Your daddy has me well protected 24/7, baby."

"I know, Ma. I still gotta check on you from time to time though."

"I know, Viviana, and thank you, baby. I love you baby girl."

"I love you too, Mama. Mama, I want you to meet this guy I been dating for a while now. He proposed to me too, Mama!" Viviana said full of excitement.

"What! Aww, Viviana, I'm so happy for you, but I do want to meet the young man responsible for stealing my baby's heart. Just call me ahead of time so I can have things prepared, like dinner and wine or something. You know what I mean, baby."

"Yes, Mama, I do, and I will."

"Aww, Viviana, I know your father would be so happy for you."

"I'm sure he would be too. I just know it. Lord, Mama, if only he were here to see it."

"I know, baby and you deserve to be happy. But call me when you decide to bring him over because Mama about to go to bed now."

"I'm sorry. I know it's late, Ma, and we will. I love you."

"I love you too, Viviana, talk to you later, baby. Goodnight." Next, she decided to call Martha.

"Hey, Chica, is everything okay?" Martha answered.

"Yes, everything is good, but I do want you to call Gloria so we all can be on a conference call together, please."

"Sure, Viv, hold on. Gloria picked up on the second ring.

"Martha? What's going on girl why are you calling me so late?"

"Hush, girl. What are you doing?"

"Oh hey, Viv. I didn't know you were on the phone too, but what the hell do y'all think I'm doing this time of the night? I'm sleeping."

"What's going on?"

"Nothing, girl, just running the deli, Gloria said.

"Good, but I was wanting the both of you on the phone because I need to know what the two of you are doing this coming weekend?"

"Nothing after we get off on Saturday," Gloria answered first.

"I'm free too," Martha said.

"Well, great, because you guys are not working on Friday, Saturday or Sunday, because I'm taking you to Italy!"

"What? Viv are you serious?" Gloria asked.

"No way," Martha replied.

"Yes way, so you ladies can pack up for a trip to Italy. I bet you thought I'd forgot about the two of you when I took my other staff to the Hamptons, huh?" she asked.

Martha and Gloria were so happy, they couldn't even reply, so instead, they just listened.

"Well I didn't forget you. I saved the best for last," she told them in an excited tone, "You two are my favorite cousins. I love y'all so much and thank you guys for everything you do."

"Aww, Viv, you're our favorite cousin too, Chica." Gloria said.

"Yes, Viv, and we love you even more."

"I just wanted you guys to be prepared for the weekend of a lifetime. I'm get off this phone for now though and I'll talk to you later," she said bringing the call to an end.

"OK. We love you!"

After hanging up with Gloria and Martha, she called Giovanni.

"Hello, babe," she said, once she heard his voice.

"Hey, baby, what are you doing?" he asked.

"I'm just lying in bed about to go to sleep, but I had to call to check on my babe first."

Giovanni had been driving, headed downtown. "Well you know what I'm doing, baby. I'm out here hustling, making this money, that's all, boo."

"That's what's up," she said. "I talked to my mother, and I told her about you. I just basically told her she would love to meet you."

"That's cool," he said, "no problem babe, but when?"

"I told her we would be by sometime this week because I'm leaving to go on a trip with Gloria and Martha. I'm taking them to Italy on Friday, and we'll be there until Monday. I wanted you to meet my mother before we go though, so that's why I called you to let you know what my plans were. I gotta keep everyone happy you know."

"Yeah, babe, I feel you."

"Gotta treat your employees right and show 'em you appreciate them. Straight up."

"Exactly, baby. Well, Giovanni my love, I'm going to let you go, baby. Be safe out there."

"Yeah let me get off this phone while I'm driving. I love you Viv," he told her.

I love you too, Giovanni. Kisses.

"Alright, kisses. Bye, boo," he repeated before hanging up.

Viviana got comfortable. She had no idea Giovanni was pulling up to her house. He had only said he was working because he didn't want her to know he was coming over. He wanted to surprise her.

Feeling restless, and lonely, Viviana rolled over in her bed under the covers. She missed Giovanni so much she held his pillow and sniffed the lingering scent of his cologne. *Damn I wish he was here*, she thought to herself, *I want him next to me... I swear I don't know what that man has done to me...*

As visions of Giovanni danced in her mind, she had no clue he was closer than she realized. Actually, he had been thinking of her all night and couldn't stand being away from her. It seemed he missed her every time he was away from her.

Viviana tossed and turned until she finally dozed off into a deep sleep, just as Giovanni walked in her room. He stood at the door and watched her as she slept. He went to the side of the bed, she was facing, and took a picture of her on his phone. *Damn my lady is so beautiful even when she is sleeping.* He stood there smiling at her before getting on his knees to kiss her lips. She was so tired she didn't feel a thing.

Smiling, he whispered in her ear, "Wake up girl…"

Viviana opened her eyes and smiled. "Giovanni, baby when did you got here? How long have I been asleep?" She smiled at him.

"I've been here for about ten minutes. I've been taking pictures of you and all and kissing you while you sleep, and you didn't even know."

"Aww, Giovanni, baby, why you do that? And I'm looking a hot mess." Viviana sat up in the bed with her hair in a bushy mess.

"No babe you don't, you look beautiful."

"Whatever, Giovanni." She said, while instantaneously patting her hair.

"No, Viv, babe, I'm serious, you look beautiful to me, and I love you so much, babe." He kissed her again on the lips.

"I love you too, Giovanni, but you are a mess for taking pictures of me. Now get in this bed with me." She pulled Giovanni in bed with her.

Viviana grabbed Giovanni's neck. "Come here to me, baby." She pulled him on top of her. "I want your loving, give it to me." "Boy, I don't know what you doing to me but it's like I can't get enough of you. I always want it all the damn time, babe," she said to Giovanni.

He smiled. "I haven't done anything but love you. The question is what have you done to me, Viv? You got my mind running in circles." Giovanni pulled Viviana on top of him. By now, he had already stripped out of his clothing, so he quickly jumped in the bed.

"I just want to love you too, Giovanni." She started moving slow on him. She took her hand and put his dick inside of her.

"Ummm, baby," Viviana moaned, as she rode him so good.

He grabbed her ass and smacked it. "Umm," she moaned. "Do it again, Giovanni. He smacked her ass again. "Umm, Giovanni I love it."

"Girl you about to make me cum riding my dick like this. This shit crazy good, girl." Giovanni's eyes rolled in the back of his head.

"I never cum this fast, damn that pussy, girl, ummm… He put his hands around her waist and started sucking on her nipples. She started riding him even faster.

"Oh, shit, Viv I'm about to explode in you baby!" Giovanni yelled out like a crazed man.

This pleased Viviana. She wanted to be in charge this go around and show him how much she loved him. "Yes, baby get that nut, explode inside me, baby," Viviana said while looking down into Giovanni's eyes, seeing them roll back into his head.

"Oh, fuck Viv, shit! Giovanni yelled as he exploded deeply inside her.

Viviana refused to let him get relaxed though. The dick was just too damn good. She used her Kegel techniques and squeezed Giovanni's hardness as if performing CPR. She smiled with satisfaction as she began to suck his lips deep into her mouth. She backed off while keeping a grip on his dick, keeping him hypnotized by her lust filled eyes. "Now give me my dick like I know you can baby," she demanded.

Giovanni flipped Viviana over and snatched her down to the end of the bed, while spreading her legs as wide as he could. He picked her up and began bouncing her up and down on him, ramming all 11 inches of his hardness inside her.

Viviana threw her head back as her eyes rolled to the back of her head as if she were in an exorcist. "Fuck me Giovanni, fuck me! I'm cummin' baby fuckkk meee . . . babyyy . . . yesss!"

Still inside her, Giovanni carried her over to the dresser, knocked all the belongings onto the floor and lay Viviana down as he proceeded to pound relentlessly inside her. "Whose pussy is this?" he asked while pounding.

"It yours Giovanni, it yours!" Viviana yelled as she climaxed all over him, gushing her juices onto his stomach and inner thighs.

the following morning...

Viviana woke up to find breakfast in bed for her with a note that read:

Good morning bae, I had the most amazing night with you last night, you're the apple of my eye. Viviana smiled while reading it. *I will spend the rest of my life showing you how much you mean to me, Viv. I love you and I've cooked some breakfast for you. I hope you enjoy it, and please enjoy your day, babe, I love you, talk to you soon,*

Love Giovanni...

"Aww. . . . Giovanni, I love you too, baby," she said aloud as she kissed the note, before beginning to eat her eggs, bacon, and toast. He'd made her a fruit bowl, and she also she had a cup waiting beside the prepared coffee with her favorite hazelnut creamer inside it, and a cold glass of apple juice.

These eggs are the bomb. I love my eggs cheesy, and he made them perfect. I'm eating like I smoked a pound of weed, Viviana thought as she noticed she had eaten everything on her plate. She got up and took her plate downstairs and found roses everywhere in her living room,

"Oh my God, I'm gonna hurt Giovanni!"

She put her plate down on the table and went over to smell the scent of the roses. *Mmm, they smell so fresh. . .* She could only smile and thank God for sending this wonderful man to her.

She continued smiling while grabbing the plate off the table and walked to her kitchen to wash the dishes. But to her surprise, her kitchen was already spotless, Giovanni had already washed everything up. Viviana looked around at everything. *Well I guess all I have to do is wash this plate out.* She quickly washed the plate, dried it, and put it in the cabinet with the rest of the cleaned dishes. She was pleased to see her kitchen so spotless.

She entered her bathroom which looked as if no one lived there. Viviana always kept her bathroom sparkling clean. Being that it was an all-white marble bathroom, she could spot a dot from the entrance. She turned on the shower and while her water was getting to the temperature she wanted, she went over to her motion-glass closet and looked through her designer wardrobe and pulled out her nude Alexander McQueen dress, with her nude Gucci belt and nude Gucci heels. *Okay, yes this looks perfect,* she thought as she laid her clothes out on her bed.

Viviana then had Alexa to start the Alicia Keys Diary track and got into the shower to enjoy the flow of the tepid water on her body. She heard her cell phone ringing as soon as she turned the water off. She rushed to get it, after draping herself in a Versace robe, but by the time she could reach it, the caller had hung up. She looked at her phone.

"Oh hell, it was Felix. Let me see what he wants," she said, out loud as she dialed his number back. "What's going on, Felix, you just called me? I was getting out the shower, what's up?

"Chillin', chillin, hustling my ass off, you know I have to keep my grind up."

"Yeah that's good. I feel you Felix."

"I'm calling to take my sexy cousin to lunch if she has time for me."

"Of course I have time for you fool. When and where is all I need to know."

"Any place you choose to go, it's my treat to you."

"Well how about Maggie's Underground?"

"You mean the one in Lakewood Viv?"

"Yes, that's the one. Meet me there around 2 o'clock okay?"

"Cool, Cuz, no problem see you at 2 then." "I'll be there Felix, bye." "Alright later," Felix said, before hanging up.

2:00 pm Maggie's Underground

Viviana was driving on the highway to Lakewood, New Jersey deep in thought. *Umm, I wonder if I should tell Felix Giovanni got locked up, and the FEDS came in my store.* She ran her fingers through her hair while waiting on traffic to move through. *Nah, I don't think so. I need to see how things pan out with him and see if I can trust him. I need to find out some more, so I'ma just keep it cool for now, just to see if he's doing any shady shit.* She shook her head, thinking about how close her and Felix use to be. *Something is very different with my cousin, it's like I can't trust him anymore.*

Viviana continued to have so many thoughts as she slowly maneuvered through the traffic. *Man, I truly want to trust him, but*

Felix has been acting really strange lately. I don't know. . . . We'll see what happens, but I hope for his sake, it's nothing fishy going on, and that it's just me being paranoid. Just as the thought passed through her mind, her phone rang. Looking down at the screen, she saw that it was Felix calling.

"Lord, speak of the devil," she said, answering the phone.

"What's up, Viv? Where you at?"

"I'm on the way, be there in like ten minutes."

"Alright, I'm waiting."

"Okay, nigga damn. I'll be there. Hold tight," she said.

"Bet, Cuz," Felix said slightly impatiently.

Ten minutes later, Viviana pulled up in her money-green Range Rover. She exited her vehicle, hitting the alarm, and entered Maggie's Underground with all eyes on her. Even couples watched her as she walked pass them looking like a lovely vision of money from head to toe. Viviana was about to call Felix, when she noticed him sitting in the back of the restaurant.

Felix threw his hand up at her to get her attention. She walked in his direction smiling. He gave his cousin a second look and noticed something different about her.

"Hey, Cuzzo, what's up with you? There's something different about you. Hell, if you weren't my cousin, I'd have to make you my main side-chick."

"Boy, give me a hug. You so crazy, but thanks for the compliment," she said as she sat down.

"What's been up with you though? You've been a little distant lately," Viviana said, while looking around for the waitress.

"You're looking like a million bucks," Felix said ignoring the *distant* comment.

"I guess this is what being in love does to a person," she said while waving her right hand in his face to reveal the beautiful ring she was wearing. "Giovanni asked me to marry him," Viviana said smiling at Felix.

"You serious, Viv?"

"Yes, so I guess you will have to walk me down the aisle, huh?"

Felix smiled. "Hell yeah, Cuz. I will. I'm happy for you, girl. You doing your thing. But I can't believe you got that serious with ole dude, Viv. I know I haven't seen you lately and all but damn girl, you got this nigga proposing to you and shit? Shit, Viv that's a big ass rock on your finger," Felix said holding Viviana's hand, staring at the ring.

"Yes, it is a nice ring," she agreed, admiring her ring smiling. "I love him, Felix. Everything I wanted in a man, he's it."

"That's some real shit right there. I'm happy to see you so happy, Cuz." He stood to his feet to give Viviana a hug.

"Thank you, Felix." She was happy to know Felix was genuinely happy for her.

"You ordered anything yet?" Viv asked as she looked at the menu.

"Nah, not yet. I was waiting for you," he said, as he looked through the menu as well.

The waitress came over to the table and asked if they were ready to order. "Hi! How are you guys doing? My name is Candice, and I'll be your waitress today."

By the way, ma'am, you are so pretty," she said, admiring Viviana.

"Well, thank you, and you are just as pretty yourself," Viviana truthfully returned the compliment to the young lady.

"You two look like a power couple," the waitress said smiling, ready to take their order with her tablet and stylus in hand. Felix and Viv both laughed. The waitress looked at them with a confused expression.

"This knuckle-head is my cousin," Viviana told her with a light chuckle. "Even if we weren't related, he's too whorish for me," she added with a full laugh.

"Oh, I'm sorry," the waitress said now directing her attention on Felix—which didn't go unnoticed by Viviana; nevertheless, she proceeded with her order. "I want potstickers, an order of your shrimp scampi, a lemonade, and for my entrée I would like the Maggie's Stuffed Chicken," she concluded.

"Okay, damn, Viv, are you eating for two or what?" Felix asked looking at Viv then back at his menu.

"Shut up boy and go ahead and order."

"Okay, ma'am for my starters, I would like the steak tips, top sirloin, please."

"Anything you want, sir," the waitress said eagerly as she tapped on the tablet.

"For my entrée, give me your fall-off-the-bone ribs," Felix requested as Candace studiously continued to tap on the device taking in his every word.

"What would you like for your two sides?" she asked without taking her eyes off of the screen.

"Ahhh, let me see." Felix contemplated while looking at the list of sides. "I'll have some loaded mash potatoes and steamed veggies, and could you bring me a Bud Light, pretty lady?" Felix flashed the waitress a million-dollar smile as he sat back and propped his elbows on the back of the booth seat. Viviana could only smile and shake her head at her cousin's flirtatious swag.

Two hours had come and gone, and they had sat talking and catching up on what had been going on in one another's lives. Now, they were exiting the restaurant, making their way to their vehicles.

"Oh man I'm so stuffed," Viviana said as she rubbed her stomach and slowly opened the door to her truck. She sat down, as Felix stood at her truck door picking his teeth with a toothpick.

"Yeah, me too, Cuz. Glad we finally got together though," he said. "But, check it, I'ma holla at you later," he told her.

Viviana rolled the window down. "Okay, Felix call me," she said as she watched Felix walk to his BMW, hoping he hadn't crossed her.

CHAPTER 14

"Hello! Mother!" Viviana yelled as she and Giovanni entered her mother's house.

"Hi baby." Paula said as she hugged Viviana. "So, I guess this is my future son-in-law. How are you, Mr. Handsome?" Paula said looking Giovanni over from head-to-toe.

Giovanni was astounded at the resemblance between Viviana and her mother. Viviana was a younger, lighter version of her mother. He gave Paula a hug. "I'm good, ma'am. How are you? It's a pleasure to meet you."

"Mama, this is Giovanni, my fiancé," Viviana said with a love-smitten smile on her face.

"You were right Viviana; he is a very handsome man," Paula said approvingly.

"Yes, Mama, I told you," Viviana stated in a matter-of-fact tone.

"Thank you, ma'am," Giovanni said, accepting the compliment from Paula.

"Oh, hush up with that *ma'am* mess. Call me, Paula, baby."

"Yes, ma'— Giovanni began, but quickly corrected himself. Okay, Paula.

"Now you two love-birds come on in here and have a seat in the family room."

"What have you been doing Mama?" Viviana asked as she and Giovanni sat on the Vivacci sectional sofa. It was evident to Giovanni that Viviana had gotten her expensive taste from her mother.

"I've been great, baby, been just fine hunny," Paula said as she sat on the matching Vivacci lounger. "So, Giovanni . . . Viviana has told me a lot about you."

With a curious look on his face, Giovanni looked at Viviana, and then, back at Paula. "Oh, did she now?" he replied with a crooked grin.

"Well not a whole lot. She did, however, tell me she's in love with you, and she can't wait to marry you."

He looked into Viviana's eyes with a deep longing. "Paula, I love your daughter the same, if not more. I can't live without her, I don't wanna have to live without her. She means so much to me, and I can't wait to make her Mrs. Giovanni Lucus," he said, never taking his eyes off of Viviana. He concluded and planted a soft wet kiss on Viviana's waiting lips.

"That's right," Paula said as if a light bulb had just went off over her head, "she also told me you proposed to her." Paula smiled proudly looking at Giovanni.

"Yes, ma'— I mean, yes, Paula, I did, and she made me a happy man when she accepted. I have to have her in my life, for the rest of my life. Your daughter is the world to me."

"Aww, Giovanni baby, I love you so much." Viviana kissed him lightly on the lips.

"Look at you two love birds," Paula said as she stood to her feet. She walked to the kitchen with a big smile on her face. "I cooked breakfast for you two, so I hope you are hungry," she said from the kitchen.

Viviana and Giovanni both were quiet, so Paula stuck her head back in to see if they had heard her and realized they were engrossed in a kiss. Giovanni noticed her sticking her head in and pulled back from Viviana.

"Yes. I know I'm hungry," he said.

"Yes, Mama. You know I want some breakfast."

Paula looked at Viv suspiciously. "I know you do, and you look like you picked up a few pounds."

Viviana looked down at herself, then back up to Paula. "Do I really, Mom?"

Paula smiled at Viviana and looked in Giovanni's direction. "Are you two giving me a grandbaby?"

"Mama stop it! Do you really think I'm pregnant?"

"Yep, I sure do. You're glowing too much."

Giovanni looked at Viviana, all smiles.

"Well, Giovanni baby, what do you think of that? My mom is usually pretty accurate on these calls. She's diagnosed a few of my cousins with pregnancy before they even knew."

"I want a houseful of kids, so it's fine by me if you are. We'll just have an early start."

Paula smiled and went back to check on the food. Giovanni kissed Viviana again with thoughts of her carrying his child. Viviana didn't think she would get pregnant that quickly, but with the way they had been going at it, she could be carrying twins.

Paula walked back into the family room where they were still standing in the same spot, locked in an embrace. "Well . . . here you go," she said, carrying the hot food to the table. "I must warn you, my mom can really cook, baby, but I didn't pick up all of her culinary skills."

"My baby holds her own in the kitchen though, Paula."

"I know she was taught to cook early, even though she never had to cook, so she should be able to make a decent dish," Paula said as she handed Viviana a glass of orange juice, and her Dunkin doughnut coffee, flavored with coffee mate hazelnut creamer. They held all held hands as Giovanni blessed the food.

Paula looked and said, "See, this is what I love, two people that love each other, giving God all the grace."

"We are always thankful to God and especially for these cheese-grits," Giovanni added jokingly but seriously. "Oh, my Lord. Baby, you gone have to learn how to cook grits just like these, or your mom is going to get tired of seeing me come over for breakfast," he said and continued stuffing his face.

later that evening back at Viviana's house

Viviana and Giovanni lay in bed together holding each other when Giovanni's phone signaled a call. He glanced at the screen. "I need to catch this call baby.

"What's going on man?" Giovanni listened to the caller and shook his head as the person on the other end spoke.

Viviana could tell it was a male on the phone but couldn't understand the full conversation.

"Alright I'm on my way," Giovanni said, then hung up with the caller. He turned over and kissed Viviana. "I've gotta go handle something real quick, baby. I'll see you later my love." He kissed her even harder and got up to put his clothes on. He kissed her again as he buttoned his shirt to leave.

Viviana got up and went down the stairs to the her office. *I might as well check on the store and see how the sales are going.* She powered on her desktop and checked the spreadsheets. "Not bad," she said, looking through everything, pleased with what she saw. She looked at the clock and knew they had closed for the day, so she called the back-office number, knowing one of the girls would probably still be there. "Hey girl," she said recognizing Sandra's voice.

"Oh hey, Viv, what's going on, how you been?"

"I'm good girl just calling to check in and see how things are going at Belladonna's with you ladies. Are you good? Do you need anything?"

"Viv, stop it girl. Liz and Tonya are gonna make sure Belladonna's is straight. We all know you need to keep a low profile right now and you don't need to be worrying about Belladonna's. We got you girl. The profits are coming in daily as always, inventory is good, we're straight. My stupid brother came by here today and purchased some stuff, trying to flirt with Tonya and Liz."

"Oh my God, that damn Felix is gonna be a hoe till his grave."

"Yes girl, your cousin is a piece of work," Sandra said laughing.

"No, that brother of yours is a piece of work." Both girls laughed. "I just had lunch with that fool yesterday at Maggie's Underground," Viviana told Sandra.

"Oh really? What was my brother up to?" Sandra asked since hadn't seen him in a while either.

"Nothing, just being Felix. You know how he is girl."

"Yes, I do know how he is and he will never change."

"Let the ladies know I appreciate you all for having my back," Viviana said sincerely, meaning every word.

"Okay. I will boo. Talk to you later, Viv. Love ya." "

"Okay, baby. Love you too, bye luv." Viviana hung up, pleased that things were going well in her absence.

Viviana was already on the jet when Gloria and Martha boarded. Gloria looked around and admired the set-up before taking a seat next Viviana. Martha was totally taken aback at how exquisite the interior of the jet was.

"Oh wow, Viv! Girl this is beautiful," Martha said, complimentary to how nice the jet was decorated—one would think they were stepping inside a townhouse. Viviana had hired the same decorator she'd used for her house, and the jet was laid. Seated comfortably on the all-white chaise lounge, she sipped on a mimosa, and she looked as if she'd just stepped out of Cosmopolitan magazine.

"Hey, Loves, it's just a gift Giovanni bought us for taking quick trips," she said, as she greeted her cousins.

"This is nice, Viv! Shit girl, I'm living the good life up in here," Gloria said, popping her fingers, and swaying her hips to the music. Then she noticed the laptop lying on Viviana's lap. "Oh, hell no, Cuzzie! Ain't no work going on this weekend," she said, removing the laptop from her cousin's lap before closing it up. "And where's the damn Acapulco Gold?"

Viviana picked up a remote, pointed it at the floor between them and a center glass table evolved from the floor filled with Acapulco Gold, Panama Gold, Black Russia, and of course, Colombian good-good.

"Now this is what the fuck I'm talking about right here," Gloria said with wide eyes.

"This is some super-star shit right here girl," Martha said, in amazement.

"Well, you girls *are* stars," Viviana replied. She handed each of them a glass of champagne filled with mimosa before and producing a bong, filled and ready to go. "Let's toast and smoke to the hardest working, most beautiful ladies I know. I'm blessed to have you both as cousins," she said, causing Gloria and Martha to look at one another and smile. "The most down to earth chicas I've ever known, who just happen to be my blood, I love you guys so deeply."

"Aww, Viv. . . .You gonna make us cry," Martha said, wiping away a tear.

"You ladies mean the world to me, and I love you both cheers!"

"Thank you, Viv, we love you too," they said in unison, like the double mint twins.

"I will fuck a bitch up about you girl," Martha said, getting up to hug Viviana.

"That's right, baby doll, you better know it," Gloria chimed in. "Now let's get our smoke on divas!"

"Okay, ladies, this is your Pilot, Ross, speaking! We are about to take off, and we will be arriving in Rome, Italy, in approximately 9 hours and 6 minutes, so fasten your seat belts and enjoy your flight!"

The ladies fastened their seat belts and began the party voyage.

"Damn Giovanni got another pilot?" Viviana said, not recognizing the voice behind the overhead speakers. "Well, let's enjoy this long flight since we'll be flying until 8pm."

"I'm glad you have us set up with everything 'cause I've never flown this long before," Martha said as she looked out the jet window.

"Well just so you both know, once we land, we have to travel by boat for an hour to get to our hotel," Viviana told them.

"Why such a long ride to the hotel, Viv?" Gloria asked.

"Because, we'll be staying at a hotel on the coastal beaches. It's known to be very romantic and has amenities none of us will ever forget."

"Okay, hey now! I love how that sounds," Martha said as Gloria enjoyed the bong.

Viviana sat back smiling, loving how she could be a blessing and make people feel so loved. She looked out the window at the clouds and thanked God.

At Naples Airport, Rome, Italy

"Wake up ladies we're in Italy!" Viviana yelled, waking Gloria and Martha.

They woke up stretching, and peered out the windows.

"Oh my God, Viv, it's so pretty here," Martha said looking out at the beautiful lights of Italy's airport.

"Yes, it is," Viv agreed. The ladies got off the plane, looking around at all the other private jets on the strip.

"Look at the beautiful water, over there." Martha continued to point the beauty out to Gloria while Viviana talked to the tour guide who would guide them to their boat. "Okay, ladies I just got off the phone with the tour guide and he said he'll be here in five minutes to escort us to our boat."

"Its fine, Viv," Gloria said. "We're just so happy to be here."

"You both deserve every bit of the time you're going spend here in Italy."

They walked to a private seating area of the airport to wait on the guide to take them to their hotel, the Belmond Hotel Caruso.

"Aww man, I think I have jet lag," Viv said as she sat back in her chair exhausted.

"We still have an hour boat ride to go. I hope they have some damn food on this boat, 'cause I have the munchies from that good-good."

"Yes, Martha. All that is included in the price of the boat ride to the coast," Viviana said, trying to raise her head up, which felt like a solid twenty pounds.

Gloria noticed how tired Viviana looked. "You look like you need to be reenergized, and after smoking all of that Colombian Gold, I'm sure we could all use a good meal."

"We'll eat as soon as get on the boat," Viviana told them.

Gloria was laid back checking out the scenery. "How much did you spend on this little get-a-way for us, Viv?"

Viviana smiled weakly in Gloria's direction. "I didn't spend nearly what you girls are worth to me, so don't worry about all of that. I just want you both to have a good time."

"What's gonna cost us is these damn international calls we'll make trying to check on our hubbies, but I wouldn't have it any other way."

CHAPTER 15

"Wow, Viv, the scenery here is simply breathtaking," Gloria said, looking out into the coast and up at the beautiful hotel. Viviana was astounded herself. The pictures she'd seen didn't do the hotel justice.

"Damn, this is amazing." Viviana looked around as they were guided off the boat one by one. She travelled a lot, and she'd visited many places, but even she had never seen a sight as beautiful as the one she was seeing now. The sun shone perfectly over the mountainside, and the clouds were as white as the snow as

"Viviana, thank you for being my cousin, thank you for being rich, thank you for getting a rich man, and thank you for loving us so much! Ooh, I was tired till I saw this spread, but Martha is about to par-tay!"

Gloria and Viviana looked at each other with shocked expressions. Martha was usually the quiet one of the bunch.

"Ma'am, all of your bags and luggage are awaiting you all in your rooms."

"Oh, thank you," Viviana said turning and looking at the tour guide.

"No problem, ma'am. Mr. Lucus was precise about the care to be given to you and the ladies while you're all here. My name is Federico and I will be your private guide while you are here."

Viviana was stunned to hear this, yet impressed more and more with Giovanni.

Upon entering the hotel they admired the marble ceilings, the beautiful marble floors, and the overall décor of the entire hotel.

"If this is a dream, Viv, I don't wanna wake up," Martha said, in awe.

"If it looks like this in the lobby, imagine how our suite is gonna look. Hurry up Martha and Viv so we can go check out our quarters," Gloria said, grabbing onto Viviana and Martha's arm.

"Welcome to Belmond Hotel Caruso, ladies." The young lady at the desk greeted them.

"Thank you, ma'am. I have a reservation for Moreno, please."

"Yes ma'am, let me check that for you. Oh, yes here you are in our penthouse suite." The clerk handed Viviana the hotel keys. "You picked our most luxurious suite, ma'am. Enjoy your stay."

"Thank you, dear," Viviana said, giving the clerk a hundred-dollar tip. The young lady's eyes widened at the sight of the money.

"No, ma'am, that won't be necessary," she said refusing the money. "It's our job to make your stay comfortable and all of your gratuity has been taken care of by Mr. Lucus."

"Damn, is there no end to what that man is capable of?" Gloria asked.

"I don't know, but I have a lifetime to find out," Viviana said leading the way to the elevator. The elevator took them straight to the front door of their suite. When Viviana opened the door, all three women gasped.

"Look at this view and how amazing this room is. It's huge," Martha said, spinning slowly around the room to take in every square foot.

"I know, the pictures really don't do it justice," Viviana said walking towards the balcony.

They were at the highest level of the hotel and the view beneath them was something right out of a movie. The sight of the coast, and the waves rolling against the rocks of the hotel was nothing less than one mesmerizing.

"Viv, look, we have an Infinity pool!" Gloria shouted out excitedly.

"Yes, I see. It makes my pool looks like a kiddie pool," Viviana said just as amazed as they were.

"Now let's not get carried away, Viv," Gloria said. "That damn pool of yours is an Infinity pool, so it looks like a Kiddie Infinity." They all laughed at Gloria being her silly self.

They returned inside just as the hotel phone rang. Viviana looked at the phone then back at her cousins. *Who in the hell could* this *be?* she wondered. "Hello," she answered.

"Hey, Boo, how is my soon-to-be wife?"

"Giovanni!" Viviana yelled happily.

"Who else would it be calling you girl? Tell me so I can have them mutilated," Giovanni jokingly said.

"Oh baby, you are so silly."

"I am so serious when it comes to my baby," Giovanni said seriously.

"I'm just shocked you called the room, and how did you know what room we would be in?"

"I just called and asked for your room number, babe, but you seriously think I wouldn't call while you thousands of miles away out of the country?"

"Well. . . I mean, you got a point there, baby, but anyway I'm glad you called. You know I was gonna call you once we got settled.

"Yes, my love. I know, but I just wanted to hear your voice. Federico told me you had arrived safely."

"Speaking of Federico, I see you went behind my back and took care of everything. You are one sneaky man, my love."

"If you think that's sneaky, come open the front door."

Viviana went to the door and peeked through the peephole. She squealed out, scaring Gloria and Martha, who had no clue what was going on.

Gloria grabbed her eggshell-colored blue Glock .42 and aimed it at the foyer. "Open the door slowly, Viv!" Gloria warned.

Viviana opened the door to find Giovanni looking sexy as ever, wearing his Roberto Cavalli jeans, Cavalli shirt, and Cavalli belt to match.

"Well, we can cancel her ass out for girl time. Hell, his fine ass just threw a monkey wrench in that," Gloria said looking back at Martha.

Viviana jumped into Giovanni's arms. "What's up, Princess?" "Your sneaky ass is what's up," Viviana said planting kisses all over Giovanni's face, while embracing him like she hadn't seen him in years instead of hours. She caught a glimpse of two figures standing in the hallway. "What the hell?" she said as she realized who the two figures belonged to. She smiled even wider as she greeted the men. She looked at Giovanni, her eyes filled with curiosity.

"So, guys. . . . I didn't know you knew my baby," Viviana said confused.

"Where's my baby?" Mike asked eagerly.

"No, wait Mike; she's inside with Martha," Viviana whispered. "I want to see the surprise on both their faces at the same time."

Viviana had them stay at the door while she and Giovanni walked into the living space where both Martha and Gloria were.

"What's going on ladies?" Giovanni asked. "Not much now that you're here to take all of our girl's attention," Martha said, slightly disappointed. She thought this was going to be a *girl's trip*, but now Viviana would be spending her time with Giovanni. She couldn't blame her, hell if James was there, she'd do the same.

"Hey, Giovanni," they both said looking at Giovanni through disappointed eyes.

"Hey, baby," James entered the door, followed by Mike. Both Martha and Gloria began screaming, running into their men's arms.

"Oh my God baby, you are the best!" Viviana said to Giovanni as she watched the ladies with joy.

"Thank you, man," Mike said to Giovanni.

"No problem, man, I know Viv's cousins mean the world to her. I'd do anything to see her happy and seeing them happy, makes her happy. So, let's all enjoy ourselves this weekend, like true stars out here, for real," Giovanni said as he popped some bottles of Armand de Brignac Ace of Spades Rosé. "Let's toast to the good life and an even better future." He held his glass up and said, "To the good life," and everyone clinked their glasses, one to the other.

By now, everyone was worn out from their flights. After a few more laughs and drinks, each couple went to their individual rooms and retired for the remainder of the evening.

The following morning everyone sat at the Island which seated as many as twelve people.

"Okay, ladies, we got the eggs on, steaks grilling in the pan, pancakes, toast, fruit, and everything looks good," Viv said, surveying the spread room service had brought up. "Let's go wake these niggas so we can all eat. All of that drinking and smoking has me parched," she said walking towards hers and Giovanni's bedroom.

"Good morning, babe," she said, leaning over to kiss him on his cheek.

Giovanni threw his arm around Viviana's neck and pulled her into bed with him. "What's up, babe, why you waking me up so early? You know a nigga hung over, right?" He asked with a sluggish smile.

"I know you are, which is why I had room service bring up plenty of nourishment. We're all hungover, so get up and let's meet the others out there to eat," Viviana said as she left the room. She knew had she stayed in there another minute, Giovanni would've wanted to get in her panties and they would've been in there another hour or two, and right now she needed some strength.

"Good morning, Giovanni," the ladies greeted him as he joined them in the kitchen.

He greeted Mike and James, with a dap on the arm. "What's up, bruh?" Giovanni said to Mike. "What's good James?" He looked over at James who was busy smacking Martha's ass.

"What's good, bruh?" They both said back to him.

Giovanni popped Viviana on her ass as he walked by to sit down at the Island. "See how he does me?" Viviana said, looking at Giovanni with lustful eyes. "Didn't you get enough of that last night Giovanni?"

"I'll never get enough of this." he said kissing Viviana on the lips. "I'm sure we all put in work last night." He looked at the guys laughing.

"Okay, now here's the plan for today. I rented a yacht for us to chill on the rest of the weekend, so let's go ball and have some fun today on the coast."

"Word bruh?" Mike asked. Man, what could be better than chilling on the water. Let's do this shit!"

"Giovanni, what am I gonna do with you? You are just too much for me to handle, baby."

"I know I am baby, and I'm gonna always be too much for you to handle, so don't forget it." Giovanni smiled at Viv. Viviana stared into his eyes, silently thanking God again for sending her this man. He reached for her hand to help her out of her chair.

———————

Everyone was chillin, laid back enjoying the sun on the coast. The wind sent a breeze flowing in the ladies' hair which caught Giovanni's attention. He was captivated by Viviana's beauty even more as he watched the wind sweep through her hair.

"This is mad crazy, bruh," Mike said, looking off into the coast waters.

"Yeah, Giovanni man, very exclusive, Fam," James concurred as he too looked off into the clear water, as the yacht sailed through Rome.

"I can't thank you and my cousin enough for this great adventure," Gloria said looking from Viv to Giovanni.

"You're welcome baby doll," Viviana smiled at Gloria, "you are all welcome, but no thanks is needed. When my baby is happy, I'm happy," Giovanni said, embracing Viviana in his arms as they looked at the scenery of Rome from the Coast.

"Giovanni, do you think we can go to Global Blue? It's a store I've seen online. They have everything, but they also sell the Gucci

Japanese Utopian wear that I wanna get for Belladonna's, and also pick out a few things for myself," she added with a grin.

"Well that's a wrap. Fellas, we may as well find a sports bar to sit at. These ladies will be busy shopping all day," Giovanni said to the guys.

"I'm down for that, my man, Mike said. Giovanni yelled to the driver to take them downtown Rome and dock the boat once there. As the driver arrived in down town Rome. Giovanni and the fellas, along with the tour guide, helped the ladies off the boat.

"Look at all these stores here," Martha said looking around at all the tourist and stores along the docking area. "They have a Sephora here also," Viv said really excited. That was her favorite skin care and make-up store. "I have to go in there after we finish shopping at Global Blue. I definitely could use some make-up."

Viviana grabbed ahold of her cousin's arms, and the women smiled like kids in a candy store. Walking in front of the fellas, they admired all the beautiful shops and boutiques down the strip. The sidewalks were filled with tourists shopping, some on their cell phones, and others, simply enjoying life.

The ladies dumped the men at the first bar they came upon, or rather the men dumped them. They passed Federico Buccellati, a jewelry store famous for having the finest jewels in the world.

"I'll be bringing Giovanni back here," Viv said as they walked by the store. "But first I want to get to Global Blue and have that order for the Gucci Japanese Utopian wear delivered to Belladonna's."

The girls made their way inside the store and came out with bags of wear for themselves, along with the receipt for the merchandise Viviana paid for, which was being shipped to Belladonna's.

After shopping, the girls were informed that Giovanni had made reservations at Mr. 100 Tiramisú, one of the finest Italian restaurants on the Coast, so they met back up with the men and headed to have off to have dinner.

———————

After eating, everyone was tired, so they made their way back to the pier and boarded the yacht to go back to the hotel.

"Goodness, my stomach is full, and I'm dead tired," Viviana said as she yawned and entered their suite. "Geesh, look at all these shopping bags." She gathered all bags that belonged to her and Giovanni and carried them to their bedroom suite.

"Girl, you nearly bought out the whole store," Martha said. She rushed over to Viviana and grabbed a few of the bags and helped her get them to her room.

"Well, it's not just our stuff, you have quite a bit yourself," Viviana told her, "so, if I bought out the store, I'd say from the looks of it, you helped me." The two laughed.

"I think we all had fun shopping," Gloria added.

"I'ma go get me a nap in," Mike said heading to his and Gloria's bedroom.

"Where you going, baby?" Gloria asked.

Mike grabbed her hand. "Come join me for a nap baby."

"Let's go and get us a nap, too, Martha. I'll holla at you later bruh," James said, giving Giovanni a dap.

"Alright, bruh, later," Giovanni said, as he went to the room where Viviana was busy putting their bags away.

"I'm sleepy bae. Come get in the bed with me and we'll put those bags away together when we wake up."

"Okay, baby, but, let me take my clothes off, you know I love to sleep naked," Viviana said while shedding out of her clothes.

"Umm, yes, I do know," Giovanni said, watching her undress.

Cuddling underneath the covers, Giovanni kissed Viviana's shoulder as he held her from behind. "You know I love you, right?" He whispered in her ear while nibbling on her lobe.

"Yes, babe, I know. I love you more," she whispered softly. Not long after, the couple drifted into a deep sleep.

"Viv, are you packed and ready?" Gloria yelled.

The men were scheduled to leave before the women and they were just about to head out. Viviana was saying her goodbyes to Giovanni.

"Yes girl, just a second, I'm talking to Giovanni! Hold on a minute," she yelled back.

"Alright, babe, I'll see you back at home, be safe," Giovanni said kissing Viviana once more before turning to leave. "You guys ready?" he asked, looking over his shoulder at James and Mike, as both men kissed their wives goodbye.

The three women stood at the door until the men stepped inside the elevator, and just as the elevator doors begin to close, Giovanni blew a kiss in Viviana's direction—she smiled and pretended to catch it, and mouthed the words *I love you more*.

"Viv, that man loves you girl, and he's got the swag of Barak Obama," Martha said as she closed the door.

"I know, right?" Viv turned looked at Martha all smiles. "That's my baby right there. Okay, ladies let's get on out of here before we miss this boat back to the airport." She grabbed her bags and luggage from her room before calling downstairs for a bellman to meet them at the hotel entrance.

10:30am at Naples Airport

"Good morning, ladies." The pilot greeted them as they boarded the jet and took their seats. "I'm Ross and I will be your pilot for this flight. How was your stay here in Rome?" he asked from the cock-pit.

"Good morning, Ross," they said one after the other. "Our stay was lovely, but we're are all ready to get back home. Thank you for asking," Viviana answered for everyone.

"That's great." He turned around and smiled at the ladies. "You ladies buckle up and relax. We'll be in the air for 9 hours."

The ladies did as instructed and buckled up. "I hope you both had a memorable time this weekend," Viviana said smiling at Martha and Gloria.

"Yes, we did!" Martha said. "We truly appreciate this trip, Cuzzie.

"I will never forget it," Gloria said as both she and Martha leaned over to hug Viviana.

"Aww, you're both so welcome. It means a lot to me that you guys had a wonderful time," Viviana said, as they took off and watched Rome become smaller from the window of the jet.

CHAPTER 16

"Attention, we will be landing in approximately two minutes at Teterboro Airport, ladies. "Welcome home. You ladies enjoy the rest of your evening," Ross announced as he landed the jet.

"Yay!" The ladies shouted out. "We're home!"

"Thank God for watching over us," Viviana said holding her hands in a prayer-like position.

"Yes," Martha said in agreement.

They exited the jet, to their awaiting limo.

The driver dropped Martha and Gloria to their homes, before heading to Viviana's house to drop her off.

The limo driver pulled up to Viviana's house, got all her luggage out, and sat it inside the door. He bid her a goodnight and told her, "Please, let Mr. Lucus know I took great care of you ma'am."

She closed the door and let out a sigh of relief to be home and she plopped down on her sofa. Her cell phone began playing Ella Mai's, *Boo'd Up, "head over heels in love, right in front of you, ain't got to look no further baby"*. It was Giovanni.

"Hey, baby," she said softly into the phone.

"Hello, my love," Giovanni's sexy baritone voice replied. His tone seemed to sound somewhat sluggish, tired. "You made it home safely, I see."

"Yes, baby, I actually just made it in and just sat my tired ass down on the sofa."

"Good. Glad you guys made it safely as well."

"Yep, we did but I just wanted to check up on you before I go have a little chat with my boys. I'll see you a little later and I love you," he said.

"Okay, baby, I love you too," Viviana said before hanging up. "Whew-weee, I'm exhausted," she said out loud as she struggled to take her bags up to her room. After getting everything put away, she decided to go take a hot bubble bath.

After soaking for what seemed like hours, she got out of the water and draped herself in a navy-blue laced Emilio Pucci robe. She went over to her dresser drawer and pulled out the canister with her pre-rolled blunts. Next, she went to the mini-fridge and took out a chilled glass of wine, before turning on the TV to catch the 11:00 p.m. news.

The news was in the middle of showing a massive shoot-out in downtown New Jersey. Viviana's eyes grew big.

"Oh no. What the hell? Oh Lord, let me call to see if everyone in my circle is OK," she spoke out loud in a panicked tone of voice.

She placed the TV on mute before speed-dialing Giovanni. His phone rang and rang, and she prayed he'd answer, but to no avail. Rocking back and forth, she lit a blunt and pulled on it hard, hoping to calm her nerves down. Allowing several minutes to pass, she speed-dialed Giovanni's number a second time and got the same result—no answer.

"Giovanni, baby . . . why aren't you answering?" she said just above a whisper. "I hope you're okay . . ." On the verge of panic, she quickly hit redial and tried him again.

"Hello babe, what's up?" the voice on the other end said. To Vivian's relief, it was Giovanni, and she could hear the anger in his voice.

"Are you okay, baby! I just saw the news. . . . There's been a massive shoot-out in down town, Jersey. Are you okay, baby? What's wrong?" Viviana asked with urgency in her voice.

"Yeah, babe. I'm okay. . . . But one of my niggas just got shot. I'll be over in a few to fill you in on what I know so far."

"Oh, no," Viviana said holding her chest.

"Don't worry about me, baby, I'm good, but let me holla back at you in a few minutes," Giovanni said, and before Viviana could even say goodbye or ask any more questions, he'd already ended the call.

When Viviana's phone rang just ten minutes later, she assumed it was Giovanni calling back, so she answered without looking at the caller I.D..

"Hello?"

"Viviana, what's up? You okay?" Sandra and Sharon were on 3-way.

"Yeah, I'm good. I'm glad to hear from you two," Viviana told them.

"We heard about the shoot-out! What the fuck is going on?" Sharon asked.

"I don't know . . . I called Giovanni and he said he's okay but one of his boys just got shot!" she informed them.

"Oh my God, Viv!" Sandra gasped.

Viviana became silent, and then, as if she'd had a sudden revelation, she snapped her finger. "Oh shit, have either of you talked to Felix? I was gonna call him after hanging up with Giovanni, but before I could call him, your call came through."

"No, we've both tried calling him, but neither of us got an answer," Sharon said.

"Damn it, man!" Viviana yelled. I pray he's OK. Let me try calling him now, hold on."

She clicked over, placing Sandra and Sharon on hold, and tried to reach Felix, without success. "Damn, I didn't get him either," she told them, after switching back over to the other line. Viviana had a bad feeling and it caused her hands to shake, and an eerie silence grew over the phone.

"Viv? Viv, you there? Sharon called out.

"Yeah, yeah, I'm, I'm here," she stammered. "I told Felix's ass to be careful. Remember when I told you how he let that nigga who bought a few ounces from him see him cut it from the whole brick?"

"Damn, Viv, I forgot all about that shit," Sandra answered.

"The sound of this shit starting to go left," Sharon added, "I hope like hell everything is good. We love our brother and we don't wanna see anything bad happen to him."

Viviana was really getting paranoid now. She was getting a bad feeling right in the pit of her stomach. "I need you ladies to come over here because we don't need to be talking over the phone like this," she rationalized with the girls.

"Alright, we're on the way," said Sharon.

"Yeah, Viv, we'll be right over," Sandra elaborated.

Viviana took her wine and canister downstairs with her to wait on Sandra and Sharon. As she sat smoking and sipping, her mind began to wonder. *Oh God, where in the hell is Felix? Why hasn't he called back by now?*

Twenty minutes later, Sharon and Sandra arrived, and Viviana rushed to open the door.

"I hope you're okay, Cuz," Sandra said as soon as she noticed the worried look on Vivian's face.

"Did either of you try calling Felix again?" she asked.

"Yep, I called his phone the whole ride over here," Sharon said somberly.

"I drove like a bat out of hell trying to get here," Sandra said somewhat perturbed, "shit, almost got pulled over by the cops."

They all sat down on Viv's sofa, as she took it upon herself to fire up another blunt. "Shit, I warned that damn Felix to be careful," she said, as she took a long pull from the blunt. It was a wonder she didn't drop it since her hands were shaking so badly. "Okay, okay, I, need to calm my ass down and not jump to any conclusions," she said as she passed the blunt to Sharon.

All the women sat silently with their heads down, each one in her own thoughts, when suddenly, the doorbell rang. Viviana jumped to her feet and walked quickly to the door to see who it was. She peeped through the peephole before opening it.

"It's Giovanni," she said, looking over her shoulder at her cousins. "Hey, baby you okay?" she asked as soon as she opened the door. She rushed to his arms hugging and kissing him, relieved to see his face.

"Yeah, I'm good, bae," he said, leading her back to the living room where Sharon and Sandra sat waiting to hear what he had to say. "What's going on, ladies?" he spoke.

"Hey, Giovanni," they said in unison. He noticed the somber expression on both their faces; however, his next question surprised everyone.

"Where that nigga Felix at?" he asked. The wrinkles in his brow and the frown on his face reflected the anger in his voice. He looked from Sharon to Sandra, and then back to Sandra again.

"We don't know, Giovanni . . . We been trying to call him for the last hour or so," Sandra said. Seemingly taken aback, she was a bit confused by his attitude.

"Yeah, babe, we've been calling his phone but no answer. What's going on, baby?" Viviana asked, more concerned now than before.

Giovanni looked at Viviana and saw the worry on her face. "Look baby, you remember the guy who saw Felix cut from the key of coke?"

Viviana began to get really nervous. "I remember, but I don't know the guy.

"Well I know him, he just shot and robbed one of my guys and I need Felix to lead me to him. I was told Felix was nowhere on the scene, so he gets a pass for right now, because he was about to be a dead man too. Family or no family, he *will* be a dead man if I find out he had something to do with this."

"No, Giovanni," Sharon and Sandra both said.

"Viv, please tell Giovanni not to kill our brother!" Sharon pleaded as if she knew Felix was guilty.

"I just pray he didn't have nothing to do with this, Sharon," Sandra said to her sister before turning her focus on Giovanni and Viv.

Giovanni got up and began pacing the floor. Viviana went over to him to try and talk rationally to him. She had never seen him angry on this level before, and frankly, it scared her.

"Giovanni, baby wait," she said softly, walking up behind him.

"What! I told you, Viv, this shit I do is real!" he said, pointing his finger in her face, "and your cousin gonna be a dead man if I find out he had something to do with my man gettin' shot! Fuck all that talkin' and shit!" he said as his tone grew louder.

"Baby, please, calm down and listen to me," Viviana continued trying to calm Giovanni down.

"No, Viv," he said in a tone that let everyone in the room know he meant business, "listen to me Viv, Sandra, Sharon . . . Y'all better find that nigga before I do and tell him to come holla at me. Since he's blood to everybody in this room, I'll give him a chance to explain to me what the hell is going on."

Giovanni grabbed Viviana's face with both hands and kissed her. "Viv, I love you, and I hope you know that, but I hate for this to turn ugly." He kissed her again, this time more passionately, harder, then he kissed the tears streaming down her cheeks before abruptly turning to leave without saying another word to anyone.

As he walked out the door, he looked back at Sharon and Sandra on their phones trying to reach Felix again. He went back in and walked up to them with sympathy on his face and murder in his eyes. "You are both cool with me, but your brother will be a dead man if you don't find him and get him to me," and with that said, he turned around and walked out the door.

"Giovanni, I love you," Viviana shouted out through sobs, but it was too late—Giovanni had already stormed out and slammed the door behind him. He knew he couldn't look into her eyes in the state of mind he was in, because surely, his eyes read murder.

After he'd left, the ladies sat in silence. It was so quiet, you could hear a field mice fart, and for what seemed like forever, no one said a word. It was evident the thoughts going through each of their minds but neither of them dare say it to the other for fear it could be true.

"Where could he be?" Viviana asked her cousins.

"We don't know, Viv," Sandra said. She ran her fingers through her hair, something she often did when she agitated.

"It's like, this shit is out of control, only God can save him *if* he is somehow mixed up in that shooting that left Giovanni's man dead, Viviana said. "I mean, damn, Felix is my blood too, so I know how you and Sharon feeling right about now; however, there's something both of you need to know about Giovanni that I haven't told you," she took a deep breath and sighed heavily.

"He was born in Columbia and he was raised there for a while, but then, he and his parents moved to the states, here in New Jersey. He knew my father very well." Sandra and Sharon listened attentively.

"He was daddy's hitman, and we all know if daddy was ever crossed, the person responsible never lived to brag about it. Well, the person who handled all of those people for daddy was and is Giovanni. Daddy's hitman and my Giovanni are one in the same.

"So, what I'm saying is love or no love for me, the murder game is embedded in him—the man is a trained-to-go killer." By now, Viviana couldn't stop the tears as they ran down her face freely.

Both Sharon and Sandra were both shocked and amazed by this new revelation Viviana had just revealed.

"We have to find Felix before Giovanni gets his hands on him," Viviana said. She paced the floor nervously, chewing on her nails.

It was 1:30 in the morning and Sharon was still trying to call Felix. Suddenly, Viv's phone rang, startling them all. Viviana quickly looked at the screen, praying it was Felix.

"Damn, it's my mama, and I know she's calling about the shoot-out that happened down there. It's been on the news, so I know she's seen it by now . . . What should I do?" Viv looked to her cousins for guidance.

"Answer it, Viv, you know she's gonna keep calling if you don't," Sandra advised her.

Taking her cousin's advice, she answered on the fourth ring.

"Hello Ma."

"Viviana, what's wrong? Are you okay?"

"Yes, Ma, I'm fine," she lied. She shook her head in frustration.

"Well, did you see the news? There was a shoot-out here in Jersey, over on Crenshaw Drive."

"Yes, ma'am. I saw it."

"Where is your cousin Felix?"

"I don't know, Ma, but we've been trying to call him, but he's not answering."

"Oh Lord, Viv." Paula was beginning to worry now.

"Mom, don't worry. I'm sure he's okay. For now, or at least until we hear something, please don't call Aunt Linda worrying her."

"Too late; Linda already called me," Paula said.

"Aww shit," Viv said under her breath, rolling her eyes in her head.

Sandra and Sharon were both hanging onto Viv's every word. Viviana took the phone from her ear and whispered, "Your mom has already called looking for Felix.

Sandra collapsed on the sofa and threw her hands up in the air.

Sharon simply looked defeated and angrily shouted out, "Fuck! Fuck! Fuck!"

"Viviana . . . Viviana . . . Are you still there?" Paula could be heard asking through the phone.

"Yes, Ma. I'm sorry I thought another call was coming through but it wasn't."

"Okay, baby. Well, try to find Felix and let me know as soon as you do. I get so worried about you all being out there in them streets. I thought this kind of stress died with Ricardo."

Paula's last statement broke Viviana's heart to know her mom was a bundle of nerves.

"Don't worry, Mama. We're fine and everything will be okay."

"Alright, baby. Take care and call me the minute you hear from Felix. I love you."

"Love you too, Mama. Bye." Viviana made sure the call was disconnected before speaking to her cousins. "We have to find Felix and we need to find him quick," she said as she sat down on the sofa with her cousins.

2:15 a.m. Saint Michael's Medical Center

Felix was in the recovery room after the surgeons removed the bullet from his shoulder. It had been a short successful procedure and he was now awake, talking to his boys who had been waiting in his room for him.

"Hey, does anyone know who the fuck came out there shooting?" Felix asked through a heavily sedated mind.

"Nah man, we all came here to make sure you were straight. We'll find out who was behind it though. Believe that," a young dude in the corner with a tapered cut said.

"If all of you niggas in here, who in the hell out looking for the pussy-ass niggas who shot me?" Felix scanned the room from one face to another but didn't wait for an answer.

"And if anybody asks about me, tell them I'm out of town on business," he ordered. "Shit, I need to call Viv; her and my sisters been blowing my phone up all night," he said. "Who got my damn phone!" Felix snapped at no one in particular.

Stones, one of his top guys reached into his pocket and got Felix's phone for him.

Viviana and the girls were still contemplating on where to start looking for Felix when her phone began rang. Looking at the screen she saw that it was him calling.

"Oh my God, it's him!" she told Sharon and Sandra. She quickly answered the ringing phone. "Hello? Felix, where the hell have you been? We've been calling you for hours." Viviana shouted into the phone.

"We who?" he asked.

"Me and your sisters, my mama, your mama, and most importantly, Giovanni."

"What? I been in surgery at Saint Michael's Medical Center. I just got out of surgery about an hour ago," he explained.

"What! What happened to you Felix?" Viviana asked filled with concern.

"My boys and me were chillin out on the stoop and these niggas rolled up on us talking shit. Next thing we knew, the niggas pulled out their straps and started shooting at us. I got hit in the shoulder, but it's all fixed up now," he assured her.

Viviana looked at Sandra and Sharon with relief. "He's good for now," she told them, relaying what Felix had said. "We'll be down there in a about 15 minutes. What's your room number?" she asked.

"I'm still in recovery, but they'll be putting me in room two twenty-two."

"Okay, Felix. You sure you're alright, Cuz?"

"Yeah, Cuz, I'm good. I'll see you when you get here. But one more thing, Cuz," he said curiously, "why is Giovanni looking for me?"

"Because it was a shoot-out in downtown Jersey on Crenshaw tonight, one of his boys was robbed and shot. Giovanni found out it was the same nigga you sold the ounces to that day when you slipped and let him see you cut it from the key. I warned your ass to be careful nigga," Viviana said, getting frustrated with Felix all over again.

"Yeah, yeah, Viv, I remember. Damn, you don't have to keep throwing that shit in my face," he countered as a quick thought flashed through his mind . . . *Maybe that nigga was behind this shit with the dudes who shot me* . . . "Yo, tell Giovanni I didn't have nothing to do with that shit man."

"Well he wants to talk to you about it and Felix it's best you go to him before he finds you because I'm really afraid of what he might do to you," Viviana said honestly.

"Don't worry, Viv, he has no reason to come after me, and once he talks to me he'll know that. Tell him to come to the hospital and I'll answer any questions he wanna ask."

"Okay, I'll try calling him but we'll see you in a few minutes, Felix."

Before Viviana could end the call, Sharon bum rushed her with questions. "So, what happened to him Viv?"

"He said him and his boys were sitting on the stoop, on the block, just chillin, when some random dudes approached them talking shit. His guys of course wasn't having that shit and it escalated to him getting shot in the shoulder. But come on, we'll find out the full story together when we get to the hospital. Let's go."

2:35 a.m.

Viv drove her Range Rover, while Sharon and Sandra trailed behind her, heading to the hospital. When they arrived, they parked in the emergency parking lot and were headed inside the hospital when her phone began playing the ring tone for Giovanni.

"Hey baby, I was just about to call you, come to Saint Michael's Medical Center."

"Why what's wrong with you, babe?" Giovanni was still shaken up about his man getting shot, so just hearing Viviana say *Saint Michaels's Medical Center* caused his heart to drop, melting the anger in his voice. "Viv, babe, what's wrong? What happened to you?"

"I'm fine, baby. Felix is here because he was shot tonight but he's doing fine. I told him you needed to see him and he wanted you to come up here. Baby, he says he had nothing to do with your man getting shot and I don't think he would invite you to come to him if he was involved. Please come with an open mind. He is my cousin and I love him dearly."

"Which room is he in?" Giovanni asked.

Viviana told him to call her when he was outside and hung up before he could question her further. She wanted to make sure she was around when the questioning went down between he and Felix.

"That was Giovanni and he's on his way up here," she announced to Sandra and Sharon.

"Viv, I hope Giovanni don't hurt my brother," Sharon said.

"I hope not either Sharon," Viviana said with a worried look on her face.

"I don't think Giovanni will make any moves before getting some answers, but to be on the safe side, I'm going to be in the room when he talks to Felix. I love Felix as if he were my brother too; besides, Giovanni just wants to find out where the dude who shot his mans is," Viviana said, trying to give them both some reassurance of Felix's safety. "That guy that Gio is trying to find is a dead man walking for sure," she added.

CHAPTER 17

The nurse had just finished giving Felix some pain medicine and another IV bag. Sandra and Sharon were both standing over his bedside while Viviana stood at the end of his bed.

"So, Felix, are you sure you don't know who the dudes are that came after you?" Viviana questioned Felix. She wanted to get as much information from him as possible before Giovanni arrived.

"I'm positive, Viv . . . I ain't never seen them cats before, ev—

"Bro, that just doesn't sound right," Sandra interrupted him. "You're telling us that some random niggas came on a block, that you and your niggas got on lock? You want us to believe you've never seen these dudes before? Nah bro, that shit don't add up," Sandra said shaking her head from side to side. She looked at Sharon and Viviana before looking back at Felix with quiet skepticism.

"Come on, Felix, what's really going on?" Sharon asked with trepidation. "You know everybody that comes through on that block. What's really going on, bro? You need to tell us if you know something 'cause, Giovanni is on his way up here right now and he's gonna want some answers.

"He's going to be questioning you with this same shit, and if it ain't sounding right for us, how the hell do you think it's going to sound to him?" Sharon said straight to the point, no holds barred. "We can't help you if you're not being truthful with us Felix," she pleaded.

"Man look, I'm telling the truth, that's all I can say." Felix's words were really slurred from the pain medication and he was fighting the sleep that was challenging his body to rest. However, he desperately needed to stay awake and speak with Giovanni.

Felix rubbed his head with his left hand because his right arm was in a sling.

Not more than 10 minutes had passed before Giovanni ostentatiously walked inside the room and kissed Viviana softly. He acknowledged Sharon and Sandra with a nod. He then casts his eyes on Felix.

"What happened to you?" he asked rubbing his hands together, while licking his lips.

"Fucked up man, as you can see," Felix said with a nod to his injured shoulder.

"Nah man, you see, my dude . . . He the one fucked up. They say he may not pull through this one." Giovanni continued to rub his hands together.

Viviana put her head down, as did Sandra and Sharon. Suddenly, Giovanni walked over to Felix, but Viviana quickly tried to grab him by his arm.

"No, Giovanni, not here babe!" she said louder than she wanted to.

"Nah, I'm cool Viv. I just want some answers, that's all." He smiled lovingly at Viviana before turning his attention back to Felix with a forged grin.

"Look, Giovanni man . . . I had nothing to do with your man getting shot," Felix said looking at Giovanni with a look of dismay.

"So, what happened to you? Why are you laid up in this damn hospital? It was yo' man that robbed and shot my dude up. So, what's good Felix?" Giovanni asked as he pulled out his Beretta 70 and put it to Felix's head.

"Hold on, hold on, Giovanni man!" Felix said with urgency. "Viv warned me to be careful and to keep shit quiet, but I didn't listen.

I didn't think this nigga would come back and try some shit like this, man. I would have smoked his ass that day."

Giovanni removed the gun from Felix's head, replacing the position in his face. He waved the gun in Felix's face and urged him to continue his story.

"I'm listening, nigga, keep talking."

"I been knowing this nigga, man. He from around the way. That's why I slipped, and I know that's no excuse, Viv," Felix said pleading his case to both Viviana and Giovanni. "He just always seemed like a common dope fiend and I never saw any danger in hi—

"Where can I find this dude? And Felix, let me be clear. If the information you giving me don't lead me to him, I'm coming back to yo' ass like a boomerang."

Viviana saw Giovanni's jaws flexing and knew he meant business. She also observed Felix sweating, although the room temperature was a comfortable sixty-eight.

"He be around. I heard a couple of days ago he said he was gonna rob these major boss niggas over on Crenshaw, but shit man, I didn't take that shit serious. Next thing I know, me and my guys are just chillin on our block and these random dudes approached us talking shit. One thing led to another, and they pulled their guns out and started shooting. That's how I got shot and ended up here. Now I'm not sure if he was involved on my block, but I know he was not with the dudes who came up to us."

"Sounds like it was ambush if you ask me. Yo man gets robbed and shot, I get shot, and all this shit happened on the same night. Come on Giovanni, you and Viv have got to see this was an ambush," Felix concluded, looking from Giovanni's gunned hand to Viviana's accusing eyes.

He knew his cousin had a soft spot for him though and would convince Giovanni to believe him. After all, they were bonded by blood. Giovanni kept his eyes glued to Felix as he concealed his Berretta.

"It's a cold, cold, world out here Felix. I'ma tell you this for my nigga and most of all, my unborn seed." Viviana looked at Giovanni with pleading eyes. Giovanni reached for her to come to him. "I love this woman with everything in me, and for her, you will have a chance to clear your name. Find this nigga and bring him to me, or I come to you and dead yo ass," Giovanni walked out the room without another word or look at anyone.

Viviana looked to her cousins then went after Giovanni.

"Giovanni, baby wait. "Something ain't right, babe, I feel it. I think Felix is lying. I know him, and he's hiding something. I know he is."

Giovanni looked at Viv intently, as he rubbed his chin. "Yeah, I know that nigga lying and when I find out what's going on, go ahead and buy your Aunt a black dress 'cause she's going to need it."

Giovanni held Viviana tightly and looked down into her beautiful eyes, which were glistened over with tears. He kissed her drenched cheeks softly.

"You okay, baby?" he asked.

Viviana looked up at Giovanni. "No babe, not right now, my right-hand man fucked up, babe. That's my blood in there, Giovanni, and it hurts to think. . . to feel. . ."

Giovanni hugged her tighter. It tore his heart up to know she was in despair like this. Felix's ass had just been given a guarantee.

Sharon peeked out the room door, and saw Giovanni holding Viviana. "They're hugging each other, I think Giovanni's gonna be alright," she told Sandra. "He just wants to find the nigga who shot his friend. Felix, you just need to find that nigga and clear your name."

Felix just looked up to the ceiling and shook his head.

Giovanni and Viv were still standing outside of Felix's room.

"Giovanni baby, I'm sorry about your friend and I pray he pulls through," Viviana said sincerely.

"Yeah, me too, but thanks babe. It's all up to God now. He's in a critical state right now, but the staff was working hard to save his life before I left to come here," he explained allowing his heart to show a much softer side than it had just minutes prior.

Seeing the pain in Giovanni's eyes caused Viviana's heart to ache. "Baby, I love you and I don't know—

Giovanni put his finger to her lips. "Ssh, we not gonna talk that way. I'm gonna be good and so are you. I got you babe. I got *us*," he said, as he rubbed her stomach and bent down as if he were kissing the baby.

Everybody in the hospital hall starred at them; one nurse, walked by with a smile. "Aww, are you two newlyweds?" she asked.

Giovanni looked at the nurse, smiled, and said, "This beautiful woman will soon be my wife and the mother of my child. I'm the luckiest man in the world."

The other nurses standing nearby began to whisper oohs and awws. Giovanni kissed Viv one last time and walked away to go check the status of his man.

Two weeks had gone by and Felix had been back and forth at his mother's house a lot more lately, especially since he was still recuperating from the bullet wound to his shoulder. When she'd heard that he'd been shot, she was scared to death. Even after learning he'd make a full recovery, she still wanted him to stay at her house for a couple of weeks. But, with lots of convincing from he and his sisters, she finally came to realize he was going to be okay. Nevertheless, she was still upset that he'd put himself in harm's way

Linda had cooked a big dinner for her son and had fixed him a huge plate. "Felix, you know you had me scared out of my mind, boy? What in the hell have I told you about hanging in those streets? Son, you need to get job, something to get you off of those streets," she lectured him.

"Ma, this looks good, you know I love your fried chicken and mashed potatoes." Felix shoved some mashed potatoes into his mouth. "Mmm, yeah, this is really good."

"Don't *mmm-ma* me. You heard me boy." she reprimanded him.

Felix knew he would have to face his mom sooner or later, well the time was now. He adjusted himself for the sermon he knew he was about to get. "Yes, ma'am, I heard you," he answered. "But, look Ma, I just got out of the hospital, I really don't want to hear you fussing at me right now," he said trying to appeal to her sympathetic side.

"Well, you're going to listen, and you will hear me Felix. It's up to you to accept what I say." Felix put his hand on his forehead. "You're my only son and I love you," her eyes began to water at the thought of almost losing her son.

"I love you too, Ma, but please don't cry," Felix pleaded. He could take a bullet, but he couldn't take seeing his mama cry.

"I get so nervous every time night falls, because I know you're out there somewhere in those evil streets, selling that shit."

Felix looked over at his mom and shook his head with a grin on his face. "Mama, I'ma be okay. I know how to take care of myself."

"Felix, I don't want anything to happen to you, that's all."

Linda continued washing the dishes with her face turned to the side so Felix wouldn't see the tears falling from her eyes.

"Come here, Ma," he said ushering her into a warm embrace.

Linda walked over and grabbed Felix and hugged him as if she would never hug him again.,

"It's gonna be alright, Ma, I promise," Felix said, unsure himself.

"Okay, baby. I love you Felix. Please son, be safe for mama," she pleaded.

"I love you too, Ma," he said, using his good hand to wipe her wet cheek. "You know I can't stand to see you cry, so please don't, Ma."

"So how is Viviana doing with her pretty self?" Felix rolled his eyes while Linda's back was turned. He knew where this conversation was leading to next. "Viv good, Ma," he said looking back at his mother.

"You know your Aunt Paula thinks Viviana is taking over and keeping Ricardo's drug operation going, don't you?" she asked knowingly.

"What? Why would Aunt Paula think something like that?" Felix asked while stuffing his mouth.

"Because she sees Viviana driving in all these expensive, fancy cars and trucks. She said every time she talks to Viviana she's either out of town or going out of town."

"Ma, you and Aunt Paula need to stop being some gossiping old biddies, and stop being so nosy," he said with a smirk. "I mean, what do Aunt Paula expect? The girl works hard, she owns several businesses, and plus she is about to marry into money."

Linda looked back at Felix at the mention of Viviana getting married. "Really, Felix? Your cousin is getting married? Paula's ass gossips about everything else, why in the hell didn't she tell me the good news. Who is he? Do you know him?" Felix laughed at his mom's excitement.

"Yes, I've met him, Ma, and she wants me to walk her down the aisle."

Linda was pleased to hear this news even more. She knew Viviana had loved her daddy dearly and to ask Felix to step in for him for such a special occasion, and it made her heart melt. Felix and Viviana had always been more like brother and sister growing up and she was happy to know they were just as close now even as adults.

"Oh yes that would wonderful, Son. "Y'all were always close, closer than you and your sisters."

"Yeah, we sure was, but Viv is mad at me right now, well not mad, but upset with me on some stupid stuff I did. But it's no problem, she'll be alright soon, she always forgives me," Felix boasted.

"Now, Felix, don't ruin your relationship with your cousin over some ole' silly mess in those streets."

Just then, the doorbell rang and Linda asked Felix to get the door. She was trying to get her kitchen cleaned so she could sit down and have some time with him.

Felix went to the door and wondered if his mother had been expecting company. "You expectin' a man to come by, Ma?" he yelled back into the kitchen jokingly.

He opened the door and his eyes became the size of the saucer he'd just eaten his dessert from.

"Who is it Felix?!" Linda yelled from the kitchen.

The guest invited herself in past a shocked Felix and walked into the kitchen where Linda was busy washing dishes.

"Hello lady, what are you doing having dinner without inviting me?" the voice asked from the kitchen doorway.

Linda looked back and threw the dishtowel down with a squeal.

"Paula!" What are you doing here? It's so good to see you. I have a bone to pick with you. Why didn't you tell me my niece is getting married? I had to hear it from your nephew here," Linda said embracing her sister.

"Well I knew he would tell you. My nephew is good with delivering news," Paula said while locking eyes with Felix behind Linda's back. . . .

To Be Continued . . .